...topped, rig... ...middle of the hallway, turned to face her.

...ally?'

...dn't glance around to see if anyone was ...ing, just put his hand on her elbow and ...ly steered her back against the wall. He ...ped in, so he could stare down into her ..., and his pupils dilated in the dim light as ...crutinised her features one by one.

...'s inner voice chanted, *Tsk-tsk. Silly girl. ...s what comes of pulling the tiger's tail.*

... voice lowered, and when he spoke it ...d her inner voice was right.

... have anything? What about you, Mia? ... have you?'

LYREBIRD LAKE MATERNITY

Every day brings a miracle…

It's time for these midwives
to become mothers themselves!

Previously single mum Montana Browne
captured our hearts in…
THE MIDWIFE'S LITTLE MIRACLE

We caught up with Misty Buchanan in…
THE MIDWIFE'S NEW-FOUND FAMILY

Now it's time to meet Mia!
PREGNANT MIDWIFE: FATHER NEEDED

PREGNANT MIDWIFE: FATHER NEEDED

BY

FIONA McARTHUR

First published in Great Britain 2009
Harlequin Mills & Boon Limited,
Eton House, 18-24 Paradise Road, Richmond, Surrey TW9 1SR

ISBN: 978 0 263 86867 8

Set in Times Roman 10½ on 13¼ pt
03-0909-40626

Harlequin Mills & Boon policy is to use papers that are natural, renewable and recyclable products and made from wood grown in sustainable forests. The logging and manufacturing process conform to the legal environmental regulations of the country of origin.

Printed and bound in Spain
by Litografia Rosés, S.A., Barcelona

PREGNANT MIDWIFE: FATHER NEEDED

A mother to five sons, **Fiona McArthur** is an Australian midwife who loves to write. Medical™ Romance gives Fiona the scope to write about all the wonderful aspects of adventure, romance, medicine and midwifery that she feels so passionate about—as well as an excuse to travel! So, now that the boys are older, her husband Ian and youngest son Rory are off with Fiona to meet new people, see new places, and have wonderful adventures. Fiona's website is at www.fionamcarthur.com

Recent titles by the same author:

THE MIDWIFE'S LITTLE MIRACLE
(Lyrebird Lake Maternity)
THE MIDWIFE'S NEW-FOUND FAMILY
(Lyrebird Lake Maternity)
THEIR SPECIAL-CARE BABY
THE SURGEON'S SPECIAL GIFT

CHAPTER ONE

'IS THIS the right place, Dad?'

Angus Campbell looked at the son he still couldn't believe was his and patted Simon's shoulder awkwardly. 'Yes, mate.' How did one learn to be a 'dad' in one weekend? Angus pushed the thought away, raised his hand, and knocked on his own father's door. 'I just needed a minute to get my head together.'

He was talking to a closed door and the lack of response was unexpected. Angus strode to the window and peered in.

The house was quiet, something he couldn't remember it ever being. When you were brought up in a country doctor's residence there was always someone coming or going. At the very least the housekeeper, Louisa, was usually there.

That would be the Louisa his father was going to marry. Another idea he had to get used to.

He turned the handle of the front door and, sure

enough, it swung open. They'd never locked the front in his time either.

He looked at Simon and then peered down the central hallway again. 'Doesn't look like anyone is home.'

His words fell away as the door to the bathroom opened and out of a cloud of billowing steam, framed by the door, stepped a very pink—and delightfully curved in all the right places—woman. And she was only just wrapped in a leaf-green towel, putting him in mind of a rose on a dew-laden morning.

Angus learned his new son was a gentleman when Simon spun on his heel and faced the other way, unlike his father.

He should really do that too. Instead, Angus met the steady green eyes assessing his arrival and unashamedly enjoyed the spectacular view. 'Sorry.'

'So I see.' Her voice was level and delightfully throaty, and she could have been dressed in a three-piece business suit given her composure. She held his gaze and he lost sight of the rest. 'Can I help you?' she finally asked.

Impressed, Angus did avert his eyes for a moment. 'I'm looking for Ned.' He looked back. Yep. Dewy rose. 'Does he still live here?'

'Ah.' She nodded as if something had been confirmed. 'The prodigal son! We heard you were coming. They've all left for the hospital to see the new baby. Give me a minute and I'll be right out.'

She slipped into a room two doors down and shut the door firmly.

Angus blinked and stepped back.

'She can handle you, Dad. Watch out.' Angus turned to look at this young man he barely knew, his son, and tilted his head.

'Really? On what knowledge do you base that assumption?'

Simon grinned. 'On my knowledge of women.'

So that explained it? The kid wasn't even twenty. 'How can you have such knowledge of women at your tender age?'

Simon flashed him a cheeky smile and Angus felt that pang again that he'd missed seeing this amazing young being grow up. No doubt he himself would have been a different man if he'd known he'd had a son. Angus felt the anger rise again and he damped it down ruthlessly. It was okay. He knew now.

Simon went on. 'Because I have four sisters and you've been working eighty hours a week all over the world since I was born.'

Angus thought of the extremely desirable women he'd dated for short periods in far-off places over the years and decided his son didn't need to know his father had more than a little experience himself. 'So you know about me and not the other way around?'

'Mum filled me in.'

Angus swallowed the bile in his throat. That would be the woman who had told Angus she'd miscarried this boy-man twenty years ago. The one woman he'd loved and wanted to marry who had married someone else.

His son went on. 'She said she had to in case something happened to her.'

Angus drew a discreet breath to remove the overtones from his voice. 'Well, I wish she'd told me about you earlier.'

Grey eyes met grey and he saw a little of his own anger in Simon's usual good nature. 'So do I.'

Mia Storm, oblivious to the amusement she'd left in her wake, shut the door firmly and leant against it. Hunk alert.

There was something about that big, craggy man at the door that sucked the breath from her lungs and accelerated her heart rate in a totally unwanted response, but it was okay. She knew it was a hormonal reaction that she could control. Would control! She was coping with pregnancy hormones, wasn't she?

She'd come to Lyrebird Lake to start anew, build a good life for her unborn child and herself, fresh and immune to the destructive hold men like him seemed to have over her.

Not precisely him, because she didn't know him from Adam, but there was that look in his eye that said he'd like to take half a dozen steps forward and carry her back into the bathroom and kick the door shut.

Her arms broke out in goose-bumps. Where the

heck had that come from? She could feel the heat in her cheeks and she stepped away from the door as if there was a blowtorch on the other side.

He was Ned's son, for crikey's sake. A man that had walked out of his father's country doctor's residence twenty years ago and not bothered once to see if dear, sweet Ned was still alive, or so her friend, Misty, said.

No doubt after he'd had his way with her in the bathroom he'd be gone from her life just as quickly as the man who'd run from the child growing inside her.

Stop it!

Nobody was having their way with anybody in the bathroom and she needed to take control. She was good at that.

Mia ripped off her towel and pulled on her briefs. Now that she came to think about it there had been two people at the door, but she couldn't remember anything about the other one except that he'd turned around, as he should, when confronted by a person undressed in their own house.

Not like…Angus. That was his name. She clipped her bra and spun it to the front. The big A, more likely. Mia stepped into her green shorts and yanked her 'Fight Breast Cancer' T-shirt over her head and glanced in the mirror.

Her hair bounced red ringlets all over her head like a frenzied mattress and she squeezed and rolled the coils so they flattened onto her head until most were confined by the elastic band in the middle. She hated the unruliness of her hair as the one thing she couldn't control.

He'd been tall so she pushed her feet into her high-heeled sandals and straightened her shirt over her slightly rounded waist. She didn't look pregnant yet.

Right, then.

She was back. He and Simon had retreated to the veranda and he'd considered going over to the hospital to look for his father because he'd behaved badly in there. He should have backed out of the door and knocked again, but his usual ease with women had been poleaxed by the vision in the hallway.

The vision looked him up and down and he saw that she was actually quite ordinary. Well, ordinary in an extraordinary way. Actually rounded and somehow…lush. Not really ordinary at all.

'I'm Mia Storm. One of the midwives. I board here. I gather you're Angus.'

She was a summer storm all right. Still in pink and green, hot as all get out one minute then drenching him with a cold shower of disdain, then blowing information at him like a gust of leaves. She looked like a militant hybrid with a rosebud mouth. She was hot!

He couldn't think of a thing to say and he had to be saved by a nineteen-year-old Lothario. It was embarrassing. And ridiculously backed up his son's impression of his father's lack of experience. If it weren't so mortifying, it would be amusing.

Simon stepped forward and held out his hand. 'I'm Simon, the son he didn't know about, and I've dragged him here to see the grandfather I've never met. You'll have to forgive him. He's still adjusting his horizons.'

Mia looked from Simon to Angus and her face softened. Simon had certainly taken the gust out of her storm and Angus could only watch in admiration. She smiled at both of them, the sun came out, and now he wouldn't be able to speak for another ten seconds. What the heck had happened to him?

'Hello, Simon.' She chuckled delightfully, Angus thought fuzzily, at Simon's ingenious explanations, and then Simon leant forward and kissed her cheek.

Angus frowned. The little upstart. As if it was the most natural thing in the world. Maybe he really had missed the boat on social behaviour.

'And does your father have your winning ways?' She tilted her head at him and somehow Angus knew she'd forgiven his faux pas in the hallway and even might feel sorry for his lack of social graces compared to his son's.

He cleared his throat. 'My apologies, Mia. I shouldn't have opened the door. I thought the house was empty.'

Simon butted in. 'Apparently Dad hasn't socialised much in the last twenty years, but he's really good at disasters.'

Thanks, son. That made him sound so promising. 'Okay, Simon. Mia doesn't want to know about me.' Angus's eyes were drawn back to hers. 'You said my father was over at the hospital with the new baby.' A thought tickled his sense of the ridiculous and he glanced at Simon. 'Not a new uncle or aunt for Simon perchance?' Serve him right. Let the upstart work out the odds for that.

This time she smiled for him. And again it was worth waiting for. 'No. Ned's a bit past having babies I think. One of the doctors here, Ben—his daughter had a child. Ned's gone over to pass a silver coin across the baby's palm.'

It was strange how nostalgic that unexpected reminder of all his father's superstitions made Angus feel. How had twenty years gone without returning to at least make peace with him?

Angus had been going to, or he'd thought of it, but there'd never seemed to be time between flights and international health disasters to get up this way. He'd been ashamed of his behaviour all those years ago and hadn't wanted a rushed trip. And after he and Simon's mother had 'lost' the baby it had been too heart-wrenching to come back in the early years.

Later it had always been the too-short breaks between missions he'd blamed. But that stood up poorly now. His father must have aged so much since he'd last seen him. 'How's Dad's health?'

'Apart from his eyesight and a stiff hip, Ned's well.' She looked into his face to gauge his reaction. 'He's well enough to marry Louisa and dance at his own wedding.'

'I'm glad. It seems I've been fortunate that it's not too late to catch up.'

She looked him up and down like a schoolmarm and he felt the dusting of disapproval for his negligence. 'Very fortunate.' Then she glanced into the house. 'Do you want to come in and wait here, or do you want to look for him over at the hospital?'

Angus needed to get over his response to this woman before he met his father and opened up a whole new bag of angst.

He didn't do sentiment, hadn't for years, but right at this minute he felt emotionally laden and he needed to shake the excess from his mind first.

This morning's first meeting with Simon, finding his son looked like a younger version of himself with better people skills and the realisation of all he'd missed out on. With its accompanying well of bitterness at Simon's mother's betrayal, which he'd had to hide from her son, and now he'd been knocked for six by the rose.

Angus lifted his kit. 'We'll put our gear inside. Then I think I'll go for a walk.'

'I'll stay here and look around,' Simon said, and grinned at Mia.

No doubt flirting, Angus thought. 'As long as

you're not too shy,' he murmured dryly to himself, as he followed his son and Mia into the house.

The room she showed Simon was positioned two doors along the central hallway from Angus's. Mia was in the middle—so next door to him. He liked that and his belly kicked as if to let him in on the reason. Okay. So maybe he did know why.

He glanced up at the high ceiling in the central hallway and memories rushed in.

He glanced into Simon's room, the one with the French doors that led out to the wide verandas. You could slip in unnoticed when needed, as he recalled nostalgically.

He remembered at least eight bedrooms at this end and the four larger rooms at his father's end where his old room was and the day clinics were held.

There'd always been other staff staying here then as well, so this end had been technically out of bounds to him as a child.

He'd stolen kisses in one of these empty rooms with Simon's mother twenty years ago. His father had been right to say that a kiss led to a lot more. He glanced at the boy beside him and thought again of all he'd missed.

'Did you want to see your room?' Mia spoke from his shoulder and he snapped back to the present day.

'Thank you, yes.'

He left Simon and followed her. Actually, he spent the two seconds observing the way her little backside wriggled delightfully, and his body just came along for the ride. Good grief. He was having an adolescent crisis. No doubt because of the memories that were crowding in from the time years ago when he'd been a raging mass of testosterone. He had to snap out of it.

Suddenly he realised the back of her lovely neck was pinker than it had been and a slow smile tugged at his lips. So she'd noticed him too. She was really going to be cross with him now.

'This is it.' She stopped, but didn't turn around, and again his mouth twitched. He had an idea she didn't want him to see her blush and he was determined he would.

'Thanks, Mia.' He didn't move to open the door and though she turned back she averted her face as she looked at a point over his left shoulder. Her cheeks were delightfully dusted with pink.

He waited, but she didn't say anything so he let her off the hook. 'I'll put the bags in and have a wander, then.'

'You do that,' she said to the wall behind him.

CHAPTER TWO

WHEN she heard the front door close Mia's shoulders slumped and she fanned her face. Whew.

Unable to stop herself she slipped into one of the empty front rooms to watch his progress through the front curtains.

Angus crossed the lawn towards the road like a man on a mission, tall and aloof with his dark hair cut in a severe military style, a man not used to being close to others. Yet she had the feeling he was able to appreciate the differences in Simon from himself, and might even be proud of his son's social ease.

As Angus turned to walk along the lake shore Ned limped out of the hospital across the road and Mia leant on the windowsill and watched—she couldn't not watch—though she didn't know why she held her breath.

Angus hesitated, then turned toward the older man, and when they were face to face Ned stepped forward and reached up to put his arms around his much taller son.

Angus's hands were slower to rise, but just as fierce when they got there. He bent and hugged his father in return and almost lifted him off the ground.

Mia felt the tears prickle her eyes and she blinked them away. This was ridiculous. Neither man was anything to her. She'd only known Ned since she'd moved here after Misty's wedding three weeks ago, and he was a sweetie, but she'd met Angus barely ten minutes ago. It was a family reunion. There was nothing to cry about.

She turned to go back down the hallway and Simon stood in his own doorway and watched her.

'What?'

Simon held up both palms in surrender then lifted one hand and physically wiped the smile from his face. 'Nothing. Nothing.' But she could see the twinkle in the eyes he'd inherited from his father and she shook her head. The teenage girls in Lyrebird Lake had better watch out for this one or there would be broken hearts everywhere.

'Go to your room.' Mia pretended to shoo him, and he laughed.

'Yes, Mum.'

Well, at least they had that pecking order sorted, she thought with a rueful smile. She doubted it would be so easy to deal with Angus.

Thank goodness she needed to get ready for work.

* * *

All was quiet at the Lyrebird Lake Birth Centre, a small midwifery-run wing of the tiny hospital that had grown to catch around two hundred babies a year.

'So Ned's son arrived.' Mia hadn't meant to blurt it out. She should have at least waited until Misty had finished handover report for the evening shift.

Misty Buchanan, Mia's friend from her training days in Sydney and one of the three full-time midwives at the unit, looked up and raised her brows. 'What's he like? I can't help feeling sorry for Ned. He's been that nervous, waiting for him to arrive.'

Mia avoided her eyes. 'I saw them hug outside the hospital so I think all's fine.' Actually, she'd sniffed at the window because a man she didn't know had hugged another she barely knew. What on earth had got into her? 'He's brought his own son, so Ned's a grandfather. The boy looks about nineteen.' Mia couldn't help smiling at the thought of Simon. 'He's a card.'

Misty smiled. 'And what's Angus like? Is he short and round like his dad?'

Mia remembered Angus's height and shoulder width and that moment she'd first seen him so large in the hallway. Not to mention the strong jaw that seemed to tug at smiling but didn't quite make it. 'Nothing like Ned.'

Misty tilted her head. 'Really? Like what, then?'

'Just a man.' Mia tried, but she'd said it far too nonchalantly to fool Misty.

'Mia?'

Misty tapped her pen and Mia shook her head. 'I am not going there.' She'd waited a lifetime to find the right man to trust her heart to, and look where that had got her.

'Well, I admit you've been burnt the one time you did.' Misty paused and glanced around to check no one was listening before she lowered her voice even further. 'But what's he like?'

Mia knew she was trapped. 'What do you want me to say, Misty? That he's tall and dark and handsome and when he looks at me I want to put my head down, hug myself and blush?'

Misty did a double-take and Mia felt like grabbing the words from the air and putting them back in her mouth. What was wrong with her?

Thank goodness she'd run off at the mouth like that with someone she could trust. Misty, and Montana, who had been the first to come to work at Lyrebird Lake, had been her friends for years and they understood each other.

They understood that Mia was still bruised from the last tall, dark and handsome man that had stirred her, promised her the world for life, and then brushed her and her pregnancy off like dust on his sleeve.

'I'll look forward to meeting him, then,' Misty said, and glanced down at the notes in her hand.

Mia felt the next glance, but she didn't meet it and her friend did what she'd hoped she would do.

'The ward's very quiet. Josephine Perry is

coming in at three to talk to you about arranging private relaxation lessons and maybe a home birth. She'd better hurry because they've only a few weeks to go. Josephine and Paul are friends of Andy's. You've met them, the flying people from the aero club.'

Mia remembered them. A great couple. 'Yep. It's their first baby. They were at the antenatal class last week.'

'Otherwise Tammy and my step-grandchild…' Misty grinned at the thought '…are coming home with me when I leave and the ward will be empty. Staff in Emergency will be glad to see you because the morning girls have left them with a full house.'

'No problem. I'll go over there as soon as I clean up here.'

'Ben's picking us up.' Misty's voice warmed again when she said her new husband's name and Mia wondered how things would be for them, sharing early married life with Ben's teenage daughter, Tammy, and her new baby.

'Tammy's still managing well?' At ten years younger than herself, Mia had marvelled at the natural way Tammy had embraced motherhood and she hoped she'd be able to cope as well when her own child arrived.

'She's wonderful. Jack's taken to feeding like a baby a month old, not just a day. We'll prepare her meals and help out for the next few weeks when she comes home, though.'

'Do you get sick of cooking now that you've left the residence for your own home?'

Misty smiled. 'Ben might when our baby comes. He cooks a lot now, though. That man is amazing. It's lovely to have our own house. Bliss! The rest of the furniture arrived yesterday. Tammy and Jack have a separate flat underneath. It's gorgeous, and she's really excited to have their own space.'

Mia couldn't help a tiny probe. 'As long as you and Ben have your own space.'

Misty smiled at some secret thought and Mia hated herself when she felt a stab of jealousy over her friend's happiness. 'We have our own space.'

Mia looked down at her now ringless hand. That should have been her. To catch babies at work, have babies at home, and find that man who would make her glow like Misty glowed now.

She'd been rudely awakened to the fact that the fiancé she'd left behind at Westside had been no great loss. It had all been such a fabulous whirlwind when they'd met. The knight to storm her chastity, romantic declarations and gifts from Mark, but then within a few months she'd been the cook, cleaner, laundress and all-round organiser for a man who just wanted a mother while he played at medical research.

She'd thought she was in love, he'd looked the part and even said the right words in the beginning, but now she just felt stupid for seeing something that hadn't been there.

The first inkling had come when she'd caught a virus that had left her weak and unable to care for herself, let alone do all the things she'd grown used to doing for Mark.

He'd been horrified that she'd hoped he'd help her. Then to find out she was pregnant when her contraception had failed and Mark's absolute horror and total denial that he would ever want a family or responsibilities. Something he'd neglected to mention when he'd asked her to marry him.

Then his other girlfriend had showed up. Another research scientist and as glamorous as Mark.

Mia wasn't sure who she felt more sorry for. Herself for love and illusions wasted or the poor woman who was engaged to him now.

She and her baby would be fine. She would build a wonderful life for both of them and Lyrebird Lake would help them.

'You okay?'

Mia refocussed on her friend. 'Sorry.' She dredged up a smile for Misty. 'I'm so glad you and Montana insisted I move up here. I've missed you guys.'

'We're glad you're here too. Apart from the fact that we desperately need midwives as our clientele grows. Come and say hello to my stepdaughter. Tammy's almost packed.'

* * *

Half an hour later Mia watched the new family drive away and she turned back to tidy up before Josephine arrived. After that she'd lock up. A couple of hours in a busy emergency ward would be just the thing to stomp on the self-pitying thoughts she couldn't shake off.

Her thoughts drifted over to Ned and Angus and she wondered how things were going over at the house. It was surprising how much she would have liked to be a fly on the wall over there.

'We missed you last night.' Angus was already in the kitchen the next morning when Mia opened the door, and he looked very large and very much at home.

She guessed technically he was home! From something Simon had said she had the feeling that his father hadn't had much of a home life since he'd left.

Angus stood up and waited for her to be seated and she frowned. She'd thought chivalry had gone out with the ark. It'd certainly had for Mark.

'Good morning, Angus. Don't wait for me. Please sit down.' She poured herself a tiny coffee from a shiny chrome percolator she'd never seen before, which was plugged beside the stove. A taste wouldn't hurt, she thought, adding plenty of milk for good measure.

'I'll wait,' he said, and she frowned at him.

The strong smell of rich coffee beans made her draw a deep, indulgent sigh and when she opened her eyes Angus was watching her. She sat quickly.

'Smells good?'

'My only weakness,' she said firmly and ignored the tremble in her knees. Then she had a thought. 'Coffee and chocolate. I have two.'

'Chocolate?'

'Mmm.' She wanted to talk about him. 'So what are your plans now you've been reunited with Ned and found a son?'

He put his cup down and sat back in the chair. The silence lengthened and he didn't smile, but somehow she knew he was amused. 'So you just want to go straight for the information, do you? No fooling around?' Angus said.

Their eyes met and she could feel those flickering darts of heat in her stomach that she hadn't realised could be ignited by just a glance. She shouldn't even be talking to this guy. He was far too dangerous to her peace of mind.

She feigned an uninterested shrug and pulled the toast he'd indicated towards her. 'If you don't want to tell me then don't.' It was so frustrating that she couldn't read his thoughts, but she didn't have any idea what was going on in his mind.

'Prickly little thing, aren't you?' was all he said.

So he wasn't going to answer. It was disappointing, but she'd live.

Then he went on as if musing. 'Should I tell you something and you can decide whether ou think it's a good choice on my part?'

She frowned. 'I was just making polite conversation.' Well, she wasn't really, because she wanted to know, but blow him. He could keep his plans secret for all she cared.

'Ah. Polite.' The inflection rose as if he didn't believe a word of it.

She glared at him again. The guy was infuriating. Then she noticed the tiny quirk at the edge of those sinfully seductive lips of his and realised.

And he confirmed it. 'So I should stop teasing you?'

She relaxed as he dragged a smile out of her. 'You had me going. I'm not used to subtlety. My fiancé has none.' She didn't know why she did it, maybe some dormant protective instinct, but she put the present tense in there as a safeguard from the feelings this man stirred in her.

'You're engaged?'

She didn't meet his eyes. 'To a doctor in Sydney.'

Angus looked interested. 'So when are you getting married?'

That's what came of telling lies. 'We're having a break.' Then she looked at him and added, 'I don't want to talk about it.' Well, that was the truth.

'Fine. Neither do I.' He did that almost-smile thing with his lips and she held her breath in case he actually did give her a full-blown grin, but it didn't happen. The guy would be an awesome poker player.

She took a sip of the glorious coffee and closed her

eyes. 'Did you make this?' Good coffee was the only thing she missed about Sydney. Even a taste was heaven.

'Yep. My specialty.' He paused. 'So what are you doing today?' he asked just as she took another sip, and her glottis closed too late as coffee slipped into her windpipe and suddenly she had to cough and splutter inelegantly as she wheezed to get her breath.

Almost immediately Angus was behind her chair and with both his hands he straightened her shoulders and then tapped her once between the shoulder blades. Not in that thumping, cure-worse-than-the-disease way men usually had, but one firm tap with the flat of his hand that cleared her airway instantly.

She whistled in the next breath and her sight cleared as she wiped her eyes. 'Thank you.'

He sat down. 'My pleasure. Next time I'll wait until after you sip before I start a conversation.'

She pushed the coffee away. She was embarrassed enough. 'I've had enough.'

He nodded. 'Then it's safe to ask again? If you have any plans for today?'

Mia didn't know where to look so she settled for a glance at the coffee pot and back. 'I'm on call from three this afternoon and doing the night shift if I'm needed in Maternity.'

'Then you could come for an early lunch?'

That's what she'd thought he was getting to. Whoa, there, boy. Didn't I just say I was unavailable?

Almost as if he heard her thoughts he went on. 'I should explain. You being engaged actually helps as I don't want to give you the wrong impression.'

Wrong impression? Didn't want her to get her hopes up, perhaps? What a poser. The man had tickets on himself.

'I'm taking my father and his future wife out for lunch today and I think Louisa would be more comfortable if there was another woman there instead of just three men.'

For the first time he looked anxious. 'I really do want this to go smoothly and I think you would be able to help that.'

Maybe not a poser? She'd have to stop jumping to conclusions about people, but Mark had left her wary. Now she understood and she wasn't disappointed that he hadn't actually wanted to ask her out. At all. Honest. 'Steer the conversation when it falters, you mean?'

He nodded. 'Something like that.'

She thought of his son. 'I don't think you'd have to worry with Simon at the table.' Their eyes met in acknowledgement of the truth of that and Mia smiled.

Angus said, 'My son is adept at conversation. I grant you that. Must be his mother's side.' A shadow passed across his face at the mention of Simon's mother and Mia couldn't help but wonder what the story was there. No way was she asking.

The less he thought about that the better, Angus

admonished himself silently, and looked up at the curly-headed nymph across the table. Unfortunately it felt like he could sit and look at her all day. She made him feel alive—not something he'd dwelt on for a long time—and she made him smile inside. Years since he'd done that.

'Nevertheless, you will come?' He didn't know why it was so important to have Mia with them, especially now he knew she was engaged, though what sort of 'engagement' had a break? The marriage didn't sound too imminent. But he did want her with them today. He barely knew her, but he had this crazy idea in his brain that he wouldn't mess up with his father and Louisa if Mia was there.

He could run hospitals, organise airlifts and troubleshoot the health of disaster-affected cities, but last night, even with Simon there yabbering away like a rabbit, he'd had trouble talking to the man who had banished him twenty years ago. And his father had been just as bad.

He watched her sniff the cup and it was funny just how much he enjoyed her obvious appreciation. Maybe he could bribe her with more coffee.

'I'll come if you think it will help,' she said when she put the cup down. 'Where were you planning on taking them?'

He'd sorted that one. 'I thought the white guesthouse on the lake. They have lunches on the veranda.'

She nodded and he guessed that was approval. 'We could walk there.'

He watched her consider that. Her thoughts flicked across her face like a digital photo frame, one after the other. How could anyone be that transparent? It was strangely endearing in a way. Then she said, 'Nice. I'll be there. What time do you want me to be ready?'

It was that easy. She'd be there. It had been Simon's suggestion and his know-it-all son had been right again. She had said yes.

He would have asked her even if Simon hadn't suggested it. He was pretty sure. 'Twelve. I'll book for twelve-fifteen.'

'No problem. I've a breathing and relaxation class this morning for a client, but will be home by eleven. I'll see you then.'

'Thank you, Mia. I appreciate this.'

She was wearing a little green sundress and when she shrugged those beautiful shoulders of hers his fingers spread on his lap as he imagined the feel of her. He'd bet her skin would be like silk. He needed to get a grip—but not on her.

Lucky his face wasn't readable like hers.

'No problem,' she said. 'You're offering free lunch at a place I've wanted to go to and with people I like. No hardship.'

Four hours later the restaurant owner settled them on the shady veranda and they could look through the overhanging branches to the lake.

Louisa had given Mia a squeeze on the arm as they'd sat down and in return she sent Louisa a reassuring nod because even if Angus didn't smile much she had an idea he was a fair and reasonable man.

Mia would make sure there was nothing for the older lady to be nervous of, though, to give Angus his due, he'd invited her for just that reason.

Ned seemed overly hearty too and Mia began to understand that Angus wasn't the only one who felt some strain with the family party.

Simon looked as relaxed as a tomcat in the sun and proceeded to nod at all the pretty girls at the other tables.

Mia couldn't help smiling at him. Then she looked up she saw that Angus was watching her and her smile faded.

No wonder it felt more like a wake than a party, with Mr Dour over there. He could make a little more effort.

'So, five days to the wedding?' Mia said brightly into the silence, and half of the table jumped at the sound of her voice.

Angus's half didn't. He just stared thoughtfully at Mia.

Ned dived in. 'I keep telling Louisa to let the caterers do the work. We're having the reception outside in a marquee, no connection to the house or the kitchen, and I can't have my bride exhausted for her wedding.'

Louisa looked fondly across at her fiancé. 'Well you had to catch wedding fever from Misty and Ben and want it all done in a month. Not that I mind.' Louisa reached across and squeezed Ned's hand.

Mia blurted out the question as it rose. 'So had you thought about staying till Saturday, then, Angus?' She hoped no one thought she had any interest in the answer, but it was too late to call it back once it was out.

There was silence at the table and Angus narrowed his eyes at Mia and then turned to his father.

'I hadn't intended to.'

Simon leant forward as if to say something and Angus raised his finger and silenced him without looking in his direction. Interesting dynamics with so short an acquaintance, Mia thought, but Angus did look used to command. Simon sat back in his seat.

Angus went on. 'I've a meeting in Brisbane on Thursday, but could fly back that night and stay the extra two days, I guess. If Louisa and you would like us to, of course.' He looked at Louisa for the first time and his face softened. 'If you'll have us.'

Angus glanced at his son, who nodded before returning his attention to his father's fiancée. Mia thought for a moment he would smile, but he didn't.

'Of course.' Louisa smiled for everyone and she seemed to relax a little. 'We'd love you to stay. I'm so pleased you can manage it.'

'That's settled, then,' Mia said as another silence settled over the table. Mentally she groaned as nobody picked up the conversational ball. This was hard work. Didn't these people know how to have a good time? She looked at Simon and mischief lurked in his eyes. Salvation.

'Tell us a joke, Simon,' Mia said, and sat back to listen.

Simon couldn't wait. 'Once there was…' And the lunch improved marginally from then on.

CHAPTER THREE

'GOOD morning, Mia.' Angus stood as she entered the breakfast room and she didn't bother to tell him to sit down. Mia wondered if she would have been disappointed if he hadn't risen. How quickly she could adapt to chivalry.

'Morning,' she said briefly.

After saying he'd stay for the wedding, Angus had said very little else at the lunch and despite Simon's jokes it had been a long and painful affair. She was still cross with Angus's poor effort, although Louisa had spoken to her later and raved about how much better that meeting had gone than the previous night.

And to think she'd wanted to be a fly on the wall the first night. No doubt the flies had left the room bored witless.

The aroma of his special coffee beans teased her nose and she sniffed reluctantly. At least he made excellent coffee and she wondered if he'd be offended if she wasted it just to sniff.

When she sat down she could feel the weight of his appraisal and she looked up and glared at him. His eyes widened in surprise and she looked away. As well you might wonder, mister, she grumbled silently to herself. Poor Louisa must dread running into him.

Who did he think he was anyway, putting a damper on the whole house? Her control snapped. 'So what happened between you and your father to make you so cold towards him now?'

One thick black brow twitched. 'You do like to dance around a subject, don't you?'

'I'm not in the mood to play games this morning, Angus. If I hadn't been called into work after lunch I would have said this yesterday. Now I've lost sleep over how upset I was for Ned and Louisa.'

He sat back in the chair and considered her. 'I'm sorry you lost sleep about something that's really not your concern.'

Snooty pig, Mia thought. Well, someone had to stick up for Ned and Louisa. 'Because it's not my concern is the very reason I can say what I like. You can freeze me out, but the cold will bite back.'

'It's all a Storm in a coffee cup,' he quipped, and she rolled her eyes.

Spare me, Mia thought. 'Do you have any idea how many times I've heard jokes about my name in my lifetime?'

His face was deadpan. 'Storm by name and storm by nature.'

She inhaled the steam and it was as good as she remembered. He'd be gone by the time she could really enjoy the stuff. 'You won't divert me. I want to know what happened between you and Ned.'

The expression on his face didn't change, but she had the feeling she'd actually penetrated the thick barriers he'd surrounded himself with. So she wasn't surprised he told her—just with the brevity of the telling, and the fact that he sounded like a bored newsreader discussing a famine he had no interest in.

'My mother left my father when I was sixteen. She ran away with another man and I blamed my father because I didn't want to blame my mother.'

'Poor Ned,' she said.

He inclined his head, but she couldn't tell if he agreed or not. He went on. 'Then I slept with Simon's mother and she fell pregnant and my father warned me she wouldn't stay with me either. After a heated discussion with my father, Simon's mother and I left, and I haven't spoken to him since he told me never to return.'

That explained that, but something still wasn't right. 'If you knew Simon's mother was pregnant, how come you didn't know about Simon?'

He raised his eyebrows. 'Because as far as I was aware he wasn't born alive.'

She thought about that. Someone had done the dirty on Angus.

He rolled his shoulders and rocked his head from side to side as if his neck was stiff, and she wondered if he'd slept at all last night either. Maybe she should offer to massage his neck. That thought started a slow burn she didn't want to think about and she took another sip of her coffee.

In all fairness to Angus, though, Mia thought, it took two to fight. 'Did Ned never contact you?'

'He had no idea where I was. For a while there in the air force I wasn't contactable anyway.' He stood up, properly filled her cup, and then carried his plate to the sink where he rinsed it.

That little action, a tiny thing that Mark had never done in the whole time they'd been together, dissolved any last remnants of anger from yesterday.

That Angus topped up her coffee, regardless of the fact she wouldn't finish it and had put a plate in the sink because it was not her job, or Louisa's, to look after him, did a strange thing to her stomach. Made her look at Angus again in a much more favourable light. Thankfully he didn't seem to notice her frozen stare.

He had to have other faults, she decided. 'Tell me about when you left home with Simon's mother.' Something he did must have driven her away. 'Didn't you know she was unhappy?'

He held up his hands in surrender. 'I must have missed it. She was pregnant! I thought she was moody from the pregnancy. But gradually I began to see I was more excited about the pregnancy than she was. I certainly hadn't expected to have a child at twenty, but when it happened I actually got used to the idea I would be a father, planned to be a good one, and really looked forward to the birth. But we had little money after bills and she missed the comfort she was accustomed to. Her parents owned the large hotel on the lake in those days. They kept telling her I was too young to look after her properly.'

'So why did you think she'd lost the baby back then?'

He didn't answer immediately, and she thought he wasn't going to, but he did. 'I never knew how it happened. Could only imagine and, of course, you imagine the worst. It started one day when she said she was going home for a visit to her parents and two days later she rang me to say she'd had a stillbirth. A son. I'd spent the last two nights painting a cot and had bought things for the baby to surprise her and now our baby was gone. Lost. And I'd never even seen him and never would. I was devastated.'

He looked at her and despite the lack of tell-tale signs she knew those memories had shaped the man.

'I think I know why most people heal better when they see and hold a child that has died. When I was in disaster areas I was just as anxious to retrieve those that had died for that reason. To make it possible for a parent to hold that child, hug them, for what was going to be the last time they had the chance to parent that child. I got none of that and I really wanted it. I wanted to see my son, but she said the funeral had come and gone.'

He shook his head. 'But Simon didn't die in utero. He was growing up with another father all the time. As far as I knew, he was gone. I've always wondered what he looked like. She told me she just wanted to forget so I thought the worst. And, of course, she didn't come back.'

'Why didn't you return to the lake to see her later?'

'She told me she didn't want me to follow her home.'

Poor Angus. To be locked out of sharing his grief while being estranged from his own family as well.

He looked away and she could see he regretted his disclosures. She hoped that now he'd spoken about them he might begin to heal. And surely it would help now he could at least begin to be a second father to Simon.

'So nineteen years later Simon just appeared?'

'So it seems. In fact, she hadn't miscarried, just met and decided on her future husband, and her pact included telling Simon the other man was his real father.'

He shrugged. 'I might not have made it back to the lake if Simon hadn't forced my hand. So here I am. Now, if you don't mind, that subject is closed.'

Mia subsided, sniffed, and her olfactory cells celebrated. 'So where…' he turned and stared her down, daring her to ask another question and she resisted the temptation and grinned '…do you get your coffee beans?'

He froze, his cheek twitched, but no smile. But nearly, buster, she thought. I nearly had you.

'Touché,' he said. 'Shades of me yesterday. You had me going then.'

She smiled into the cup. 'Yep.'

'You realize, of course, it's your fault I'll have seven days in Lyrebird Lake.'

'Your choice.'

'Your suggestion.'

Mia shrugged. 'I just said you should. You don't know me from Adam.'

'Oh, I think I'd know the difference between you and Adam.' He looked her up and down and suddenly she remembered her thoughts of him that first day he'd arrived. The bathroom, she could feel the steam on her skin, and hear the sound from the door that he'd kick shut with both of them inside. She could feel the heat steal up her cheeks and a sudden flutter in her stomach made her push out her chair in a sudden ungainly rush.

His voice followed her to the door. 'So what are you doing this morning?'

Brain? Where was her brain? Then it began to work again. 'I've a breathing and relaxation class with a new couple.' Thank goodness for the excuse, she thought.

'Breathing. I'm very interested in that. Did my obstetric rotation years ago and there's something very special about the moment of birth, especially a calm one.'

Where was this going? Mia thought warily.

She'd been right to be wary. 'Any chance of tagging along to listen?' Angus said. 'One of the medics at the base and his wife rave about breathing.'

Her stomach dropped. What a load of rubbish, she thought as she paused with her back to him, but could she think of a single good reason why he couldn't come? Nope. She sighed. 'I'm leaving at ten o'clock on the dot.'

'This is Angus. He's Dr Ned's son and works for the government in disaster relief.'

Angus held out his hand to Paul, and to Mia's surprise he even smiled at Josephine. 'I hope you don't mind me listening in. I'm very interested in Mia's relaxation theories.'

Paul shrugged easily. 'No problem. The government, eh? I'm up at the mine. Site manager. My wife Josephine is a schoolteacher. Do you fly?'

Angus nodded. 'Mostly helicopters, or nothing bigger than a twin, anyway. What about you?'

Paul looked proudly at his wife. 'Jo and I met at the aero club. She restored her own Tiger Moth and I fly an Auster.'

The smile Angus showed them was the most genuine Mia had seen. 'You both fly rag and tube aeroplanes? That's great. Love to come up with you one day. Maybe you'd like a trip if the chopper comes down tomorrow. They'll be dropping me back late afternoon and we could go up then.'

'Paul can go.' Jo looked down at her tummy ruefully. 'I'm too fat to climb into helicopters.'

'Maybe I'd better not go.' Paul looked forlorn at the chance the treat might go away and Jo shook her head.

'You go, but if I go into labour while you're away I'll kill you.'

'When are you due?' Angus checked his watch for the date, as if Jo would have the baby then and there, and they all laughed.

'You've got two weeks.' Jo patted her stomach. 'So you should be fine.'

He looked at Mia, who wasn't quite tapping her foot, but glanced at her own watch, and he stepped back. 'Better fade into the background.'

'Sorry, Mia.' Paul smiled easily. 'You know what we flying types are like.'

Not till now. 'Obviously friendlier than other types. I've never seen Angus so animated,' she said dryly.

The flight bonding session seemed to be over so Jo led the way into the sitting room where they sat around a low table.

Mia put some charts down and tried to put Angus's presence into the back of her mind. How dared he be so friendly to these people he didn't know and not to his own father?

She needed to get over this and concentrate. It

wasn't her problem. She'd done this antenatal spiel dozens of times, believed it passionately, and could carry it off even with him sitting there. She knew she could. 'Let's get started, then.'

Angus clasped his hands on his lap and tilted his head like a teacher's pet. She'd kill him later.

She concentrated on Jo. 'In labour you have subconscious resources,' she began, and thankfully her voice wasn't too wobbly with those unexpected nerves. 'Resources our bodies use outside our control. Like our heart rate—around eighty beats a minute usually, but it can increase to a hundred and twenty or more if we're emotionally upset or scared.'

She couldn't help the quick glance she shot at Angus, the perfect example of someone who seemed capable of creating a fight-or-flight response in her, even when she didn't want one. She looked away before he saw her, and hurried on.

'Like thinking about labour and getting palpitations?' Josephine said, and Paul squeezed his wife's hand.

'Or thinking about the fact that Jo wants to have a home birth instead of one in the hospital.'

'Exactly.' She smiled at Josephine and Paul for allowing her to refocus on the discussion. 'Your body is served by two main nervous systems, the fight-and-flight adrenalin sort when you're uptight and scared, and the relaxation response endorphin when you feel safe and calm.'

She paused and the couple nodded, so she went on. 'Because you can't release both adrenalin and endorphin at the same time, can't be alert for danger and relaxed at the same time, you need to learn to choose relaxation as the way of stimulating the response to keep you calm. Then you can allow your labour to progress efficiently and as painlessly as possible.'

'I'm all for that,' Josephine said, 'and it wouldn't be bad for Paul to learn for when I ring my mother long distance. He definitely gets pain then.'

Mia giggled and saw that even Angus's lips twitched. 'It's a skill you can and should use for life,' she went on. 'During a relaxation response your blood vessels dilate, in pregnancy your uterine blood flow is improved and your baby is happier, and pregnant or not your breathing slows and you're ready for sleep or daydreaming.'

Paul looked fondly at his wife. 'She's like that most of the time.'

'You're just jealous, Paul,' Mia teased. 'I'll show you how to do it too. This is where we talk about mindset and breathing.'

Angus watched her, still with polite attention, but she felt he watched her lips form the words more than he heard what she said. It made her aware of the way her mouth moved, of any facial expressions she used, and her whole body seemed more alert and awkward than usual. She closed her eyes briefly and recentred herself. She could and would ignore him.

'Relaxation is helped by lots of things. You can imagine a perfect place. Maybe that place is under a tree, under a sky full of stars or on a deserted beach. Similar to that feeling you have towards the end of a really wonderful massage and you know your arm would just drop back if someone picked it up and released it again.'

Unless it was Angus who'd just massaged her, then relaxation wasn't the byproduct she'd be left with. Damn it, she needed to concentrate.

Her voice lowered. 'Just the feel of someone stroking your back, gently and rhythmically, or warm water running down your body, backwards and forwards in an unending stream, all these feather-light sensations produce endorphins.'

She saw that Paul had taken Josephine's hand and was absently stroking her fingers as he listened. Confidence grew within her. These people would be perfect for this.

Angus's grey eyes had darkened almost to black when she glanced his way and when he stared back at her she felt suspended in the moment, trapped by the messages she couldn't help but read—that he desired her.

Boom—adrenalin shot through her, and she hurried on as all the hairs on her arms stood up. 'There's a limitless supply of calming endorphins available in your body to make you more and more high on their morphine-like properties.' She tried to keep her voice calm and mellow. Where were the endorphins now? All she wanted to do was squeak and run away.

'There's litres of endorphins, in fact,' she said, a little too firmly, 'if you practise to stimulate their release.'

'I feel relaxed already, just listening to you.' Paul looked a little less sure that this relaxation was all rubbish and Josephine gave him an approving, good-boy look.

Mia bit her lip to hide her sigh of relief. So everyone couldn't tell Angus had just turned her into a quivering jelly. That was good. 'I'm glad, Paul.'

She forced herself to turn to Angus. 'How about you, Angus? Feeling relaxed?'

'Actually mesmerised.' And he didn't sound as if he was joking.

Mia frowned. It wasn't the answer she'd expected, and her brain froze inopportunely before she could go on. 'The next thing you can do is change your breathing.' Mia liked to leave breathing until she'd set it up because most people were still uncomfortable about practising something they'd done every day since birth.

'When you're ready, close your eyes. Just try a deeper breath in through your nose.' She needed a few herself at the moment to calm the flutters that had started again.

'Through your nose. Suck in air as far as you can. Imagine that breath tickling little receptors down at the bottom of your lungs that release endorphins.

Your breath actually switching on release valves. There should be maybe six to eight seconds of inspiration with practice. It takes some practice.'

She checked Paul and Jo who looked as if they would explode if they didn't breathe out soon. 'Now breathe out for four to six seconds, this time breathing out slowly through your mouth.'

Everybody opened their eyes to check they'd done it right. She smiled at their eagerness to pass the test. 'That's great. Let's try it again.'

They all breathed in. 'Now, as the breath flows in, push your belly out.' Paul looked confused for a minute and she could tell he was trying to force his belly out all the time.

She clarified. 'Notice now that when you breathe out your belly goes in.'

She watched Paul and Josephine as they both concentrated on her instructions. Angus watched her and she steered away from him. 'Now imagine doing that while in the bath or under that tree in your mind.'

Nobody spoke and everybody breathed in and out slowly. Practising. Mia peeked under her lids to see Angus doing it too. She'd assumed he'd be silently mocking during the lesson and she was glad he wasn't. But it certainly shouldn't have mattered as much as it did.

'That's great. You should practise this as much as you can before labour, Jo. Get Paul to sit down with you, maybe after tea at night.'

'The clever thing is that when you actually have your baby, right at the end, when you push, that belly pressure on the in-breath will gently birth your baby without the horrible, hold-your-breath, chin-on-your-chest-and-push pressure you've all heard about.'

Paul looked up. 'You mean I can't yell "Push, push, push" like on the telly?'

'She'll breathe your baby out, Paul. Calmly and steadily.'

'Oh, wow. I like the sound of that,' Josephine said, and her eyes met Mia's. She nodded. 'We'll definitely work on this.'

CHAPTER FOUR

AFTER the class Angus and Mia walked back along the lake to the residence and the sunlight diffused through the trees overhanging the path so that the main heat of the late morning was held off.

Mia broke the silence. 'At least you participated and didn't just sit there.'

Angus glanced down at her. She knew he did, because she felt it even without looking at him, which surely wasn't normal.

'Did you think I wouldn't join in?' he said.

Why was staying calm with this man so hard? 'Well, you were certainly friendlier with Paul and Jo than I expected.'

His voice washed over her and the thread of amusement bristled her more. 'Compared to my conversations with my father, you mean? But then you have such low expectations of me, Mia.'

Did she? She thought she was beginning to have the opposite and needed to stop that right now.

'Hmm. I'll try not to.' She turned to look up at him and his face was expressionless. As usual. She'd like to penetrate that reserve of his at least as easily as he penetrated hers. In fact, it was really unfair she couldn't.

'So what did you think?' she asked.

'I'm not sure I believe someone can breathe a baby out,' Angus said. 'All the births I've seen there seems to be a lot of exhausting chin-on-chest pushing with held breath.'

Mia nodded. 'That's what we were taught. It's sad nobody told us earlier, but the knowledge is more widespread now.'

Angus shook his head. 'I'd have to see it.'

'Do you see a cow holding its breath to push? Or a cat or dog? They breathe their babies out. Practise on the toilet, push out your belly and breath in when you go, and save yourself haemorrhoids.'

He grimaced. 'You midwives are so earthy.'

She laughed out loud, glad she could make him feel uncomfortable for a change after the way he'd been affecting her all morning. 'So what's Simon doing today while you're out sharing relaxation classes with me?'

'He and his grandfather have gone fishing.'

She glanced at the lake through the trees and then back at Angus. 'You don't like fishing?'

She saw the surprise in his face. 'Anybody who grew up on the lake likes fishing.'

Angus said it as if she should have known, but

now she was even more confused. He must have seen that too so he elaborated without her having to ask. 'I wanted them to have a chance to get to know each other.'

Men! Hello. What was he afraid of? 'Angus! You should be there. It's not like you know them both so well you didn't need to go.'

'They seemed happy to go without me.' He said it simply, but stopped in the middle of the path and she stopped too. He looked down into her face, stared intently into her eyes so that she could almost see herself reflected there, and she couldn't look away. 'You really do like to fire your home truths at me, don't you, Mia? Barbs out. No mercy. Why is that?'

She recognised a fleeting glimpse of hurt behind his eyes and suddenly she wished her words back. 'I'm sorry. As you said before, it's none of my business.'

That she wanted to pierce his reserve was no excuse for being rude, or to cause him pain. She'd never have done that to Mark, and Mark had deserved it. Angus didn't. 'I'm truly sorry, Angus. You're right.'

He looked so surprised she had to smile and add, 'I'm always leading with my mouth. I say what I feel and it just comes out.' She looked up at him darkly. 'Unlike some people I know.'

He almost smiled. 'You do lead with your mouth. It's one of the first things I noticed about you. Your beautiful, beautiful mouth.' His lids lowered over suddenly darkened irises, and she knew instinctively and exactly what he was thinking for the first time. Then she felt that rushing, tumbling-down-a-well feeling she'd felt the first day she'd seen him in the hallway.

As she stood beside him under the trees, those few seconds before he moved seemed to last a hundred heartbeats and quite clearly she could hear the birds calling to each other in the branches above, could smell the scent of a flowering shrub beside the path and feel the breeze brushing gently against her skin.

What was it about this man that seemed to tune her senses with just a look?

His face closed in, very slowly, until finally he blocked out the mottled sunlight and right before he kissed her, with his lips only an inch away, his finger came up and brushed her lower lip, as if he just had to allow himself the luxury.

He brushed her mouth softly, reverently, as if her lips were composed of the most precious silk in the world, while his fingertip slid across, backward and forward, and she melted right there in front of him with those strokes of infinite tenderness.

His other arm lifted to curl gently around her neck and he pulled her close so that their bodies came together as their mouths touched. Slowly the pressure grew firmer and she forgot everything as she sank into a place she'd never been before, a place that started soft and warm and intoxicating and grew to hot and hungry and wild and finally desperate, and totally inappropriate for a path at Lyrebird Lake in the middle of the day.

They both stepped back at the same time.

She had no doubt her shock was written all over her face, but he looked unfazed.

'Mia?'

What had just happened? She struggled to right her world that had been fully ordered yesterday, even this morning, but it continued to fade to that sensation she so desperately wanted to return to.

Not now. Not with him. She couldn't do this. 'I don't want to talk about it.' Then she said something really stupid. 'Remember I'm engaged.' And took off down the path.

Angus sighed as he watched her go. What the heck had he done that for?

He eased in one of her relaxation breaths he'd learnt about this morning because right now he sure as hell needed a little calm. He'd never kissed a woman who hadn't asked for it before and a kiss had never felt like that.

He wasn't the pirate type, but she had a way of bringing out his baser instincts like no woman ever had.

He'd been happy on his one-man island and now this curly-headed witch with her wicked mouth had tempted him out into unfamiliar waters. Waters he didn't want to venture into.

But she tasted so damn fine and her lips were to die for and the bones under the silk of her shoulders trapped him because they felt even better under his hands than he'd imagined.

Hell! He'd come back here to make sure Simon met his grandfather and in some way compensate his father for his own tardiness by doing that.

But now he'd kissed Mia on this damn path that had led him astray twenty years ago and all he could think about was how he could get Mia back in his arms. And more.

He was mad.

Then he saw the residence ahead and Mia's footsteps had slowed as her first headlong rush petered out and he caught up with her.

What he saw in her face made him want to smooth the worry lines from her forehead.

'You okay?'

'Fine,' she said shortly. 'Just leave me alone, Angus.'

He looked around and decided against the house. He spun on his heel and walked back the way they'd come. He needed to find some impossible reason he could use to get out of staying here for another three days till the wedding and then to forget how Mia had tasted and felt under his hands. Maybe he'd think of something while he flew up to Brisbane tomorrow.

That afternoon Mia was glad to get to work. She hadn't seen Angus again and as had seemed more common lately the ward was busy when she walked in. Good.

Misty was in the process of weighing a red-faced

baby and the newborn waved bunched fists as she roared her displeasure.

Mia felt the first smile she'd managed since leaving Angus that morning and glanced across to congratulate the new parents.

'This is Pedro and Giselle,' Misty said, 'and their new baby, Isabella.' She turned to an older couple who were beaming at each other in the corner. 'And these proud grandparents are Angelo and Antoinette,' Misty said. 'They own the best Italian— actually the best restaurant, in town. Their new arrival is the first girl in their family in two generations.'

Mia smiled and congratulated everyone and between her and Misty they settled the new addition and her mum into the ward for the night before attempting the ward handover.

Mia intercepted several curious glances, but avoided Misty's non-verbal cues to open up. It seemed her present state of mind was blatantly obvious. The trouble was she didn't know how she felt herself let alone wanted the risk of having one of those blurting sessions she'd taken a bent to lately with Misty.

'So how was your lesson with Jo and Paul?' Misty sat back with a sigh as she finally caught up with the paperwork.

'Was that only this morning?' No wonder today had seemed so long. 'Fine. I'd forgotten about that.' Mia could see Angus with his eyes shut, breathing in at Jo's house, that enigmatic expression daring her to guess what he was thinking.

Funny how all she could remember about the morning had to do with Angus.

Misty tilted her head. 'What else have you packed in? You seem a bit distraught. You're not having tummy pains or anything?'

Mia froze at that thought and her hand crept guiltily over her stomach. 'No.' Misty's comment grounded her like nothing else could. Her baby was the most important thing and Angus was nothing in comparison.

But he could be important. The random thought would not be silenced and she sighed.

'Nothing's wrong. Or everything.' She was hopeless and she needed to vent and maybe Misty could help.

'Something else. Or someone else?' Misty voice was quiet and the question at the end held no pressure to answer.

'Is it that obvious?' Mia sighed. 'I've only known him three days. How can he take up so much of my thoughts?'

'Angus.' Misty sat back in her chair. 'I see. Well, I'd only known Ben for a few hours and he changed me. It can happen.'

'But Angus is only here until the wedding,' Mia said, 'and then he'll be gone, and I'll be back feeling sorry for myself again if I'm not careful. I had everything worked out. I have to think of my baby. I can make a good life for the two of us here.'

Misty nodded. 'You're right. It would be sensible to be careful. Have you told him you're pregnant?'

'No.' Mia sighed. 'Well, there's the thing. I told Angus I was still engaged.'

'Oh, what tangled webs…'

'I know. Stupid idea. But even from the beginning I felt threatened by Angus.'

Misty's brows drew together. '*Threatened*'s a big word. And I thought you said he was too quiet.'

Mia shook her head. 'I said dour, but he's just reserved. With a subtle sense of humour, and if anything is going to get under my skin that will. I'm just not used to it in a man.'

She thought about that one explosive kiss and couldn't help the warmth that stole over her. 'He has his moments,' she mumbled, and dragged her mind back to work. 'So tell me about your day.'

Now that she'd finally got something out of her, Misty wasn't ready to be sidetracked.

'I'll have to meet this paragon. Invite him up to meet Ben. Maybe have Montana and Andy as well and Ned and Louisa. We're both off now until after the wedding. We could have a barbecue pre-wedding party because Louisa has refused a hen's party and Ned laughed when Ben hesitantly offered a buck's night. That way I get to meet your Angus the night before the wedding.'

'He's not my Angus.' Mia didn't want to think about a barbecue. Or trying to hide how Angus affected her in front of her friends. She'd talked about this disaster enough.

'So how's Tammy going at home? Is the baby settled?' Stepdaughter and step-grandson diversion. That worked.

Misty's eyes lit up. 'Perfect. Ben's so proud of her.'

Simon sidled up to Mia the next morning as she ate her toast. 'I thought you and Dad were getting on well?'

Mia tilted her head and answered carefully as she wondered what this was in aid of. 'As well as two strangers get on. I suppose so. Why?'

'Because something's happened and Dad doesn't want to talk about you any more.'

Hooray! 'You could take that as a sign.' Mia pretended to frown. 'Your supreme confidence that you can say anything can be a disadvantage, Simon. Has anyone told you that?'

'Dad tells me to be quiet all the time.' He said it so philosophically that Mia had to smile.

'You've obviously missed that in your life.'

Before she could say anything more the door opened and Angus walked in, and it was as if the air was sucked out of the room at the same time.

Mia consciously drew breath until she'd over-expanded her lungs, and held it before exhaling unobtrusively. Her brain started to work again now that it had oxygen. How could just seeing a man leave you oxygen starved?

Angus hesitated when he saw her, but then continued to the stove.

Simon looked at both of them and after obvious thought he slipped from the room. Mia considered going after him, but didn't. She'd never been a runner.

She pulled her plate closer. Inhale. Exhale. She'd finish her toast and go.

'Coffee?' Angus turned to face her briefly and the aroma of the freshly ground beans tickled her nostrils. She sighed. She was so weak. And not only about the coffee.

'Yes, please.'

He finished grinding and poured the water on top then plugged it in. 'I'm sorry I distressed you, yesterday, Mia.'

She noticed he didn't say he was sorry he'd kissed her. She thought about that. Was she sorry he'd kissed her or just for the turmoil it had caused in her mind? Hmm.

'I'm sorry you distressed me, too,' she said.

Grey eyes met green and this time she could see the twinkle of amusement in his eyes. 'So you enjoyed it as much as I did, then?' Still Angus wasn't smiling.

Enjoyed was too tame a word. Stunned, staggered, shocked—all words that would work. 'I guess you're pretty good at it, any girl would have.' She shrugged. 'Do you share that experience often?'

Angus felt his mood lift and the heavy lump that had been pushing down on him since yesterday eased. 'Not for a while.'

It was hard to believe he'd only known Mia for three days. Well, technically four.

It seemed he'd slipped back into the routine of the town already. The old walk along the lake path and kisses under the trees with a gorgeous woman—when had she changed from simply beautiful to gorgeous?—and now this lack of direction, apart from wanting to head for the bedroom. He hadn't suffered with this confusion since he'd left.

'I still don't want to talk about it,' Mia said. 'My thoughts haven't changed.' She gave him a strange stare, as if psyching herself up to say something, and he couldn't help the tension that eased into his shoulders. How could this woman affect him so much physically with just a look?

Then she said it, and he'd been right to tense for a shock.

'I'm pregnant, you know. My baby is due in six months and I'm a single parent. The father wants nothing to do with us and actually deposited money in an account for me to "get rid of it." I'm actually unengaged. That's why I don't want a casual affair, Angus.'

'How will you manage?' A stupid thing to say and he regretted it as soon as the words left his mouth, but thankfully she didn't look fazed by his doubt.

'We'll be fine. I'm a woman, aren't I? And I have

my friends and my job and Lyrebird Lake.' Mia jutted that determined little chin of hers and he wanted to scoop her up and tell her not all men were like that, but she went on. 'I'll make a good life for my child and myself.'

He could see the strength in her. Feel it vibrate from across the table. Mia would be aware of the hardships ahead, but looked happy to meet those hardships head on for the sake of her baby. Something Simon's mother had never been able to do.

Back then it had all been Angus's fault they were pregnant, not a shared progression in their relationship, or even regret she'd forgotten her pills and not mentioned it because he always used protection. She'd worried that the town had been talking about them, and it had been Angus's responsibility to keep her in the manner to which she'd been accustomed. And in the end it seemed she'd decided he wouldn't do a good enough job and had chosen someone else who would. Deviously.

He'd decided for his own safety that all women would be like Simon's mother and had never looked for depth in a relationship.

Obviously some were different. Now he knew why she only seemed to sniff his coffee. Pregnancy. He poured her a half shot to roll in the cup.

Mia looked at him strangely and he wondered if he'd done something wrong.

'Thank you. You saw I don't drink it, Angus?' She

said it as if no man had done such a small service for her before, and he wondered if her fiancé had done anything for her.

'So tell me what you did when you were on your own again after Simon's mother left?'

Mia loved probing, Angus mused, but somehow from her he didn't mind. Why was that? 'Questions again?' he said.

'If you feel like telling me.' She threw the comment in as if he'd believe her. Yeah, right. He felt like snorting at that. Well, she was like other women in that. As if she'd stop if he didn't want to talk about it.

Then he said something he hadn't planned to say. 'I'll tell you if you spend the day with me today.'

CHAPTER FIVE

THERE was a moment's silence while they both digested his suggestion and he reassured himself it was a good idea.

He'd spent most of last night in his bed fighting against his attraction to Mia, again rehashing the kiss on the path, telling himself he was a fool if he let himself care about someone else, but in the end he'd accepted that he couldn't think of a good enough reason not to follow his libido, because that was the best way to get it out of his system.

No use thinking long-term and no doubt it would all go nowhere fast, but it couldn't hurt to spend some time with her. And time was running out before he left Lyrebird Lake.

He'd never met anyone who could slip under his guard like this curly-headed, pregnant—he reminded himself—temptress. At least a taste. He sighed. Did he even want to get involved? Unfortunately, yes!

Mia frowned. 'Don't you have a helicopter coming down for you today?'

At least she hadn't said no straight off. 'I thought you might like to come for the flight. I'm being dropped in the middle of Brisbane. I've a two-hour meeting and final wrap-up to present and then I'm free.'

She didn't say anything and he went on, 'You could shop while you wait and we could do lunch and be back before dark. I promised Paul a quick flight late this afternoon.'

She tilted her head as if trying to understand what he offered. 'And if I do, you'll tell me what I want to know?'

He shrugged. 'Just think about coming with me today. We'll talk over lunch. There could be fascinating stuff for you to drag out of me.' He added, 'Or not.' But he was pretty sure she'd be disappointed.

Mia didn't know what to think. He'd asked her to spend the day with him right after she'd told him she was pregnant. Wasn't a woman pregnant with another man's baby the world's biggest turn-off? Or did he think he was safe because she'd have low expectations?

'Have you made plans already for today?' he said as he glanced at his watch, and she wondered just how much time she had to make up her mind.

'No, not really. I was going to wash my hair.' She'd been going to try and straighten her hair to see if she could practise for the wedding. A hair straightener in her inexperienced hands was always a bad hair day.

He glanced at his watch again. 'They'll be here in half an hour. Would that give you enough time to get dressed, with lunch in mind? I could get my PA to make you an appointment at the hairdresser's and you could be pampered for a change while I'm in the meeting. I'd give you my mobile number so we can meet up afterwards.'

'Why are you doing this?' She peered at him as if trying to see an ulterior motive.

'It's only the hairdresser's and lunch.' He tried not to think about the fact that the lunch he was proposing was in the same hotel as his suite. 'The hairdresser is my treat for upsetting your routine.'

She shook her head. 'Not the hair.'

'Doing what, then?'

'Pressuring me to come.' She narrowed her eyes. 'What's in it for you?'

He sighed. He had no idea.

Mia saw it even though she didn't hear it, and she realised in a flash that he actually didn't know either. Strange how that made her feel better and helped her decision.

She'd go. It would be fun and certainly different. She was a Sydney girl and hadn't been to Brisbane before. Big cities were fun and the idea of someone else battling with her curls was an attractive one. 'Don't worry about it,' she said. 'If I've only got half an hour I'd better move.'

She took the tiniest sip of her coffee, resigned to waste it, for the good of her baby. She stood up. 'I'll be as quick as I can.'

She heard the helicopter well before she saw it, and glanced into the mirror one final time and shrugged. A scrunched-up ball of hair on her head would be a lot better than looking like a clown after the ride.

The front door of the residence was open and she could see across the street to the hospital helipad. The chopper sat there like a huge beetle, waiting. They hadn't turned off the engines yet and she wondered if they would. She'd read somewhere pilots didn't like taking passengers on with the rotor going, but all the best movies had people ducking on their way to the cabin.

As she walked up the hallway the noise made her want to put her hands over her ears. She guessed that was normal because Angus stood to one side of the chopper, gesturing to a man in camo without trying to be heard. He looked across as she walked out the door and waved and she couldn't help the little smile that pulled at the corner of her mouth or the warm feeling his welcome gave her.

She'd known him less than a week and already her body recognised what made it feel good. The thought clanged with comprehension and her step faltered.

As if aware of her indecision, Angus left the man

and crossed the road towards her. As he came closer she could see the crease above his dark brows. 'You okay?' he mouthed.

Was it too late to back out now? Before she could think of an excuse, he took her hand and held it in both of his, and the feel of his skin against her was warm and compelling like the look he gave her.

'Choppers are perfectly safe,' he said above the noise. 'They have a great record despite what you read in the papers.'

She looked down at his hands holding hers. 'It's not the helicopter I'm afraid of,' she muttered to his shoes, and then looked up at him. He gave her a little cajoling tug on her hand again and she was lost.

She followed him across the road like a little puppy, she thought with disgust, and allowed herself to be fitted into a flying jacket and headphones.

She was mad. Exposure to a man who hourly became more attractive to her and was due to fly out of her life in three days' time was the last thing she needed. Setting herself up to be miserable when she'd promised she'd never let a man make her miserable again.

She glared down at the safety harness Angus had fastened across her chest and waist. That's what came from being weak. It was insidious. It started with coffee, then they took over your thoughts and then you couldn't say no to them. She knew where that led.

The roar of the rotors increased and the cabin

vibrated and she knew they were about to take off. It was too late. She'd made her bed so she may as well lie in it.

A flicker of warmth stirred in her stomach. Where had that thought come from? Better to not think of beds. They didn't have beds in hairdresser's or restaurants.

The thing was, she'd begun to imagine far too often since that kiss of being tangled horizontally in Angus's arms, and for a girl who'd been accused not that long ago of being less than accommodating in her love life, it seemed out of character.

The evil twin within her suggested maybe there was some truth to the idea that sex could be really fabulous and not just the pleasant diversion it had been with Mark. She'd wondered what all the fuss was about and judging by her own response to Angus she just might find out.

Angus tapped her on the arm and at some stage he'd strapped himself in next to her. She'd no idea how she had missed that, except that her dark and dangerous thoughts must have been deeper than she'd realized.

He mouthed, 'You okay?' again, as if it she might have changed her answer since last time, and she just nodded and looked out the window away from those all-seeing eyes of his.

She'd be fine once she got home this evening with

her virtue intact. Interesting point. Did pregnant single mothers have virtue?

Actually looking out the window was pretty distracting as they rose and she was happy with that. She could see the hospital on her left and as they lifted higher she could see the house and the town on the edge of the lake. Funny how the shore was almost shaped like the lyrebird it was named after.

Misty had said something about a myth and apparently she and Ben had seen the lyrebird one day, but Mia hadn't caught a glimpse since she'd been here. It could be a nice, safe topic to ask Angus about at lunch.

The ground rushed away beneath them and she decided that as she was here she may as well enjoy the flight. It wasn't every day a girl got to ride in a helicopter with a handsome man and his uniformed friends.

The flight only took an hour and she'd been fascinated by the bird's eye view over the mountains and then the outer suburbs of Brisbane before they landed at the base.

They were met by a large black SUV and the deference offered to Angus made her wonder just what sort of position he held, seeing as he wasn't technically in the armed forces.

Mia looked him in the eye. 'So who are you that men in suits pick you up in dark cars?'

'They're picking you up too.' Angus seemed a tad wary with his answer and she became even more suspicious.

'Stop avoiding the answer.'

He shrugged. 'I work for the government and I've been to interesting places.'

Uh-oh. Her stomach dropped and she knew it had all been too good to be true. 'Like a hitman?'

He actually laughed, albeit a short laugh, but she nearly missed his answer in her surprise at his blatant display of emotion. 'I'm a doctor,' he said. 'I've taken an oath not to harm. But I've grown good at negotiating.'

She frowned again. 'Now I find that ironic when you say you need me to help you make conversation with your father.'

'Ah. But I'm emotionally involved with my father. Big difference. I'm not so good at that.'

She needed to think about that and the ramifications of falling for a guy with the ability to be good at getting what he wanted. Unless he was emotionally involved, though, her Pollyanna side said, so maybe not clinically focussed on negotiating all the time. 'So where are we going now?' she asked.

'I'm dropping you at the hairdresser and because it's joined to a large shopping complex you should be well diverted for the time I'll be away. I'll phone you when I've finished and we'll have lunch when you're shopped out.'

So he had her little woman's morning organised with military precision, but she could see his mind was elsewhere and she accepted it for the moment, which was unlike her. Then again nobody had actually tried to arrange amusements for her before. It was cosseting in a sweet way, and she wasn't used to that either. What the heck. A change was as good as a holiday.

Angus dropped her at the hairdresser and Hugh, a short, busy-fingered delight who instantly put her at her ease, shampooed, massaged and gave her delicious herbal tea. Then he stared over her shoulder into the mirror and considered her hair.

'You sure you want it straight? You look gorgeous as is.'

'Straight, Hugh, please.'

He pursed his lips and nodded. 'No problem.' And it wasn't.

When Angus met her outside the maternity shop three hours later his eyes widened, but he didn't give away what he thought and she was darned if she was going to ask like some needy teenager. Well, she hoped she could hold out.

He seemed distant, though, more than usual, and looked at her a couple more times. With nothing said, he relieved her of her bags and directed her into a taxi. No discussion on the new Mia, no comment on the bags, so she bided her time until the taxi pulled up beside a green square of park between two old buildings.

One had modern signage that proclaimed the Casino and the other, discreetly, The Treasury.

When he took her into the ornate splendour of the grand hotel she forgot his aloofness, and her hair for the moment, and gazed around in pleasure. 'Wow.' Gauche perhaps, but to the point.

Bow windows overlooked the park, ceilings soared to intricate plasterwork, and ornate French provincial furnishings stood against sandstone walls. They passed gilt cabinets with Fabergé figurines, huge dark oil paintings of cattlemen and horses, and racks of beautiful plates and vases.

A senior hotel employee smiled and murmured as he passed them, 'Good to see you again, Dr Campbell.'

'You too, Liam.'

Mia craned her neck to watch the man walk away. 'Come here often, do you?'

'I have a suite. It's where I stay in Brisbane.'

Didn't he have a home? 'Where you bring your bevy of beauties?'

Angus raised his eyebrows in disbelief. 'Do I look like I'd have a bevy of beauties?'

This new Angus did. Oh, Lord, yes! She didn't know what to think. This day had not turned out as she'd imagined. She was seeing new sides to Angus she hadn't expected. They were daunting and the voice inside chanted she was out of her league and that she didn't really know this guy.

She slanted a glance up at him as they walked

along the long corridor. 'At the moment you look like you could have anything you want.'

He stopped right in the middle of the hallway and turned to face her. 'Really?' He didn't glance around to see if anyone was watching, just put his hand on her elbow and slowly steered her back against the wall until it was cold against her shoulders. Her heart skittered with the suddenness of his movement. All she could think about was that he was going to kiss her again...and she couldn't wait.

He stepped in so he could stare down into her face and his pupils dilated in the dimness as he scrutinised her features one by one.

Mia's inner voice admonished her. Silly girl. That's what comes of pulling the tiger's tail.

His voice dropped, and when he spoke it seemed her inner voice was right. 'I can have anything? What about you, Mia? Can I have you?' Then he took a strand of her straightened hair and twisted it around his finger and tugged it. 'Very pretty. But not you. I don't like it.' And he didn't kiss her. Just caressed her bottom lip with his finger and stepped back. Then he steered her away from the wall and whisked her into the restaurant so that her cheeks were still flushed when he introduced her to the maîitre d'.

'Miss Storm, Johnson. She works with my father.'

A special understanding seemed to pass between the two, and the older man nodded, smiled and bowed his head to Mia. 'I'm pleased to meet you, Miss Storm, and to hear that, sir.'

Johnson led the way to the table. Mia's head was spinning and not just from the almost-kiss.

What had happened then? That nuance-laden conversation between the two men was no fleeting restaurant relationship. It spoke of understanding, mutual respect and long-standing friendship. She'd ask about that and not think about the way her heart was still thumping.

Johnson led them to what was clearly the best table, a table in its own alcove overlooking the park, and held her chair out for her.

He smiled kindly down at her, as if aware of her curiosity. 'The doctor and I go back a long way, miss.'

He placed her napkin tenderly across her lap and passed the menu gently, as if the folder were fragile.

She seized on the new topic as the man walked away. 'So Johnson knows about you and your father.'

'Straight for the meat as ever, eh?'

Everyone knew the best defence was attack. She didn't want to think about her own weak response to the recent danger in the hallway and he didn't look too uncomfortable. The question was valid. 'You said you'd tell me anything.' But why did it seem so important to understand? 'So?'

Angus glanced around the restaurant. 'This is where I worked before Simon's mother left me.'

She frowned. 'As a waiter?'

'Does that seem so strange?'

She flicked a look at the young men in black trousers and cummerbunds. 'It's not how I imagine you.'

He raised his eyebrows. 'But I learned to make great coffee.'

She had to smile at that. 'Now I believe you. And Johnson was here then?'

'He took me under his wing.' Angus glanced across at Johnson and because she was learning to read his inscrutable face just a little, she could see the affection he held for the older gentleman. 'It was Johnson who suggested medicine in the air force when Simon's mother went home. And he's been nagging me for years to make peace with my father.'

'And why didn't you?' She leant on her elbow and gazed into his face.

'A lot of harsh words passed between my father and I.'

There was more. Mia leaned her chin on her hands. 'I though it was about the pregnancy. What else did you and your father fight about?'

'Mainly about me not starting med school.' He shrugged as if it was all too long ago to bother talking about. 'That when I left I was throwing away my scholarship on a woman who would leave me and I would amount to nothing.'

He shrugged. 'He got the woman part right, but I'd always known medicine was where I was headed, and

I couldn't wait till I graduated and could show him. But it was harder than I expected to go back and say it.'

He scrutinised some distant point over her left shoulder. 'I always seemed to want one more area of expertise under my belt before I went home and showed off, then suddenly the air force wanted some payback for all the money they'd spent on me and I wasn't in Australia much for the next few years.'

'How long have you been freelancing for the forces?'

'Five years,' Angus said, as if it wasn't long.

Long enough to figure out your priorities, she would have thought. 'So you would have accumulated decent wealth and stature and still you didn't look up your father?'

He didn't meet her eyes. 'I wasn't willing to invest in emotions when my job depended on being unemotional.'

This was becoming too mysterious and a little more daunting than she'd expected. Some job. 'Just what do you do?'

He chose his words carefully. Or at least to her it seemed so. 'I go into countries and help retrieve injured citizens and bring them back to Australian hospitals.'

Apparently not on scheduled flights. 'Is it dangerous?'

He glanced at her, but she had no hope of gleaning anything from his expression. 'Sometimes the countries they are in don't want to give us access to them.

I've worked closely with special units, accessed difficult-to-reach areas, and mostly been successful.'

She didn't want to think how often he'd been involved in dangerous missions. Didn't he realise that everyone was mortal? 'Was it a good career choice?'

He nodded. 'I think so. Post-grad in trauma medicine led me to the medical side of disaster management and the adrenalin rush replaced the urge to be a family man very quickly.'

He'd taught himself to be self-sufficient. Not unlike herself, really. But it was lonely, she knew from personal experience, except that now she had Montana and Misty. And he had Johnson.

He must have read it in her face. 'Don't feel sorry for me, Mia. I can make a difference to a few people in trouble, move on and do it all again.'

No emotional attachment, no strings, she thought. Since Simon's mother? 'So are you on leave now?'

'I've been offered another contract that involves a permanent move overseas, but I've missed out on so much with Simon I'd like to spend some time with him.'

'You do realise that you've missed out on about the same amount of time your father missed out on you.'

His brows drew together. 'I hadn't looked at it like that, but you're right.'

Her voice dropped. 'Ned won't be here for ever.'

He frowned. At least it was some outward expression of emotion. 'Thank you for pointing that out.' His tone told her she'd crossed the line again.

'I'm sorry.' She wasn't. He needed to think of Ned now. 'It's none of my business.'

He captured her gaze and held it. 'I think you say sorry very easily. Now I'll ask you something.' He paused. 'Does the man whose baby you carry think you used the money and that you're not pregnant any more?'

So what if he did? 'He might if he cared enough to think about it.'

He looked away from her and a coldness seemed to settle over him. 'All women are devious.'

'All men are bastards,' she retaliated, and he looked back in time for her to see that his eyes flickered in shock.

'Sweeping comment,' he said.

She raised her brows. 'But it's okay for you to generalise?'

He looked at her, hard, and then away. 'What would you like to eat?'

Actually, she didn't feel like eating at all, but then she lectured herself on sensible eating in pregnancy. 'I'll have the soup.'

'Nothing to drink?' Was that sarcasm? She didn't know, but she'd certainly stirred him up. It would probably do him good, she reassured herself.

'Is that a trick question?' Did he think she cared so little for her baby that she would drink alcohol?

He sighed. 'I meant a beverage, not alcohol.'

Okay, then. Truce. 'Lemonade, please.'

Johnson appeared and took the menus and orders, and Mia looked away. How had the conversation between them become so bitter in so short a time? Because she'd pried too much? Or because Mark thought there was no baby, like Angus had when Simon had been born? What did she expect if she poked at someone's wounds?

She didn't have the right to judge Angus. 'I'm sorry if I've upset you with my questions, Angus.'

He did that neck roll thing again and she realised how tense he was, but there was no sign of it in his voice. 'I agreed to the inquisition. But let's talk about something much more interesting. Tell me about you. Where has Mia Storm come from? Was your childhood rosy?'

'That's not part of the deal.' She didn't care, really. Anything to lighten the tension that sat between them.

He actually smiled at her and now she knew why he didn't do it often. Killer smile. Women would be prostrate on couches everywhere. She felt breathless and hot and incredibly fortunate to be the recipient. It was ridiculous for one little smile to have that effect on her.

'But you'll tell me anyway? Please, Mia.'

She had to laugh. She was like putty in his hands. Hopefully he couldn't tell how malleable she really was. 'I survived. My parents divorced when I was three. My mother seemed to have a problem distinguishing between reliable men and reckless ones. I became very self-sufficient. Too self-sufficient to need a man around until one day I realised that all the good ones had gone. So I wasn't going to rush into an affair with an unworthy one.'

She'd had no single women friends she'd felt close to either. 'The first really sensible women I met were during my midwifery training when I ran into Montana and Misty. I saw Montana was so happy with her first husband.' She frowned at the memory. 'Before he up and died on her, that is.'

Angus raised his eyebrows, still amused. 'Surely he didn't mean to die?'

'Hmm.' Still, it had been very inconsiderate of him, but now Montana seemed even happier with Andy. 'Anyway, for the first time I began to think that maybe I too could find a man and be happy. Maybe even have a family of my own one day.'

Angus still looked interested. 'So what happened?' he said.

'As it turns out, I'm as hopeless as my mother in picking men.'

Angus watched her talk, the food arrived, and he saw the self-deprecating humour to disguise the pain, saw the hurt of betrayal from her ex-fiancé, and he wanted to stretch across the table and hold her face and tell her she was amazing. Because she was. To him. She was vibrant and strong and, despite her ridiculous straight hair, incredibly beautiful to him. He realised that he really did have it bad and there wasn't a lot of choices to make now. Just the important one.

Would she be better off with him, or worse? He pushed away his plate. There was no choice. He was an emotional cripple and she wallowed in emotion. It would never work.

He just needed to get her out of his system. Dispel the myth that they had a chance.

CHAPTER SIX

MIA stopped talking and looked at him with those big green eyes of hers, as if she expected an answer.

'Sorry,' Angus said, 'I was watching your face and lost track.'

She frowned at that, but couldn't really be offended. 'I said, what do you know about the lyrebird myth at the lake?'

He blinked and played the question back. He remembered something his father had mentioned a long time ago, but couldn't pin it down. 'Something to do with unexpected visitations? You'd need to ask my father that. It's his sort of thing.'

He reached across and captured her hand because he had to. Wanted to stroke those slim fingers of hers and hold them again like he had that morning. 'Is that why you moved there. For a myth?'

'No.' She looked at her hand in his, then darted a glance to his face and away again, but she left her fingers in his and he could feel the heat build between them.

He fought to remember what they'd been talking about. 'Is it a place you'll stay? Lyrebird Lake?'

This time she met his eyes and he saw the decision and finality. 'Absolutely. My friends are there and the way our unit works is why I did midwifery in the first place.'

He stroked his thumb along her wrist and she pretended it didn't affect her. He knew she was pretending because the fine hairs on her arms had risen and he released her slowly because it wasn't fair to do this to her in a public restaurant. No matter what she was doing to him.

He saw her breasts rise with a deeper than normal breath and he wondered if she was enjoying her calm breathing, as he was.

The conversation at least was normal. 'The unit provides family-friendly birth,' she said. 'I'm hoping to set up my own home-birth practice in the area.'

A change of subject was probably a good idea, but he doubted any topic would remove his brain totally from his arousal. 'Isn't home birth going out on limb?' He could see the passion shining in her eyes and he hoped she wasn't going in blind.

Actually, he hoped he wasn't going in blind because he desperately needed to kiss her and they needed to get out of here before he reached across the table and did it in front of the restaurant patrons and Johnson.

'Times are changing,' she said, and he switched his thoughts back to the topic at hand. 'Lots of midwives have home-birth practices,' she said. 'With great success.'

Who was she trying to convince? he wondered.

She went on, 'If I integrate my care with the hospital, it's easy. Andy and Ben are getting used to the idea, thanks to Montana and Misty.'

'They all seem very happy.' He couldn't concentrate on what she was saying. Couldn't think of anything except how he was going to get her up to his room. He glanced around and caught Johnson's eye before he looked back at her. 'Have you had enough? Would you like dessert or another lemonade?'

'No, thank you.' She blinked at his abrupt change of topic, but he couldn't help that. 'What time are we being picked up?' she asked.

'Three.' Johnson approached with the bill. 'Excuse me,' Angus said, signed and put the number of his room on it then looked back at her. He really shouldn't go there.

'So you said you have a suite here? Permanently?' She sounded nervous. So was he, which was ridiculous.

'Hotels are easier and I've never needed a house. Before.' He watched her frown and she tried hard to resist asking. Of course she couldn't stand firm and that made him feel even more indulgent towards her than he already was. Which he wouldn't have thought possible.

'So why do you need a house now?'

He was beyond teasing her. 'I'm thinking of Simon. As a father I need a house my son can come to. And it would be nice to have somewhere to show you now, but all I have is a hotel balcony that overlooks Brisbane's Southbank. But it's a great view. Would you like to see it?'

His eyes met Mia's and the heat that crossed the table left her weak at the knees and she was glad she was still sitting.

'I could make you a herbal tea?' he said, though she had no doubt a hot beverage was the furthest thing from both their minds.

He stood up and she knew what she was agreeing to when she nodded. She just hoped her jelly legs didn't collapse on the way.

The lift had old-fashioned concertina steel doors that meshed together in diamonds and when they closed she realised there was no going back. The space inside was so small that their shoulders touched—or maybe they would have touched in a bigger lift anyway, because they seemed to be magnetised together as they stood. Even in the lift everything was exotic and luxurious, like the hotel carpet plush beneath her feet and the lift buttons that glowed dully in old ivory, like piano keys.

When the doors opened the corridor was as wide and high-ceilinged as everywhere else, and he steered her to the left by her elbow, a warm touch that seeped up her arm like a promise, until he stopped at a heavy wooden door.

He glanced down at her and must have seen what he needed to in her face because he leant forward and pushed open the door to allow her to precede him. 'Please make yourself at home. There's a bathroom through there.'

A bathroom. Good idea. She could face herself in the mirror and ask what the heck she was doing. 'Thank you.'

The bathroom was all black-and-white tiles and black speckled marble. The bath was bigger than a family-sized refrigerator and the vanity stretched for miles along one wall. She jumped at her reflection and then remembered she'd straightened her hair. But it was her eyes that told the story.

Far too many mirrors told her the same thing.

Her eyes glittered with the need for Angus to kiss her again. Wanted to be held in those strong arms and was happy to let what would happen… happen.

Foolish? Yes.

Could she change her mind? No. She didn't want to.

She didn't look at the tiny bulge of her stomach and turned away from the straight-haired woman in the mirror who wasn't really her. Somehow that made it easier.

When she returned to the other room she could smell coffee and it brought familiarity to an unfamiliar place. Then there was Angus, tall and inscrutable, gorgeous, waiting for her. Waiting on her.

He smiled and heat swamped her. 'Come and see the great view. I've even found chocolate to tempt you with.'

He'd set a table with herbal tea for her and coffee for him, and fancy chocolate shells on the balcony and she chose a milky white-chocolate cone shell, still beaded with cold from the fridge, before she moved to stand beside the stone balcony. 'You're right about the view.'

She could see across the river to the arts centre and upriver past the bridge. Boats and River Cats crisscrossed seemingly at random. The cold chocolate slowly melted in her mouth and she could feel the heat from the afternoon sun on her skin. And then she could feel his hand on her shoulder and suddenly she didn't want to think about decisions any more.

She gestured with her hand. 'This is amazing.'

'You're amazing.'

She shook her head. 'No. I'm useful, organised, usually not impulsive.' She wasn't anything special.

'That's what I find amazing.'

'I'm not sure that's a compliment.'

'Be sure it is,' he said. 'Where did you get such negativity? Come here and let me kiss you.'

Did she want him to kiss her? Of course she did and she wished he'd stop talking about it and do it, and this wasn't a bad place because they couldn't do too much on a balcony. Could they?

The pressure from his hand on her shoulder increased and he turned her to him. Then she looked up into his face and it was good to just study him. To wallow in the incredible desire for her she could see in his beautiful grey eyes, to marvel at his high cheekbones and strong chin, and really appreciate his mouth with the steep edges of his lips and curved fullness reminding her of the wonderful sensations last time. To anticipate what he'd feel like now.

'You're only a little thing, you know,' he mused as he stared back at her. 'I could put you in my pocket and carry you with me all day.' He kissed her forehead gently and pulled her against him. 'I think I'd like that.'

'I'm not sure I'd like to be in a pocket all day,' she murmured, suddenly at ease with him, no doubt as he intended, but she didn't care. It was liberating to feel relaxed enough to press her forehead against his chest and absorb the solid strength of him. To lift her chin and press her nose into his shirt and inhale the masculine scent of some expensive aftershave he'd splashed around. Which made her think about Angus, shirtless, shaved and splashing, and the heat in her throat ran to her belly like a too-hot mouthful of Angus's coffee.

Her hands came up and she undid the top three buttons on his shirt, suddenly unconcerned with the fondling etiquette, and she slipped her fingers in to savour the warmth and strength of his neck and throat. The heat inside her flickered and licked around her rib cage.

'Maybe you could keep me in your shirt pocket,' she said softly, and stroked his neck again. 'That seems a lovely place to be.'

His hand came up and he tilted her chin towards him and held it as he lowered his face closer.

'Mmm,' he said, and then there was no more talk. Just his mouth pressing down and the stroke of his tongue as he guided her mouth open. Angus did things with kissing she'd never felt before. He didn't plunder, but supped, and stroked and merged with her so that while she lost herself she found him and it was a gift. No power play like Mark, no demolishing of boundaries because everything she gave he gave back threefold, and she drifted in a timeless place as they gifted each other in a cocoon of their own making.

When he lifted his mouth her eyes opened a millisecond before his and she was able to watch him lift his lids and even gently run his tongue over his lips, as if savouring the last touch and taste of her before he gazed back. Never had she felt so appreciated, so completely kissed, so in need of more.

His hand drifted to hers and picked up her fingers and lifted them between their bodies and flattened her fingers against his chest.

'This could be dangerous.'

'I know,' she said.

'I'm leaving on Sunday.' His words were there,

but such was the glow they barely rated. This moment was real and Mia had no wish to be denied.

'I know,' she said.

Then he kissed her again and this time the heat exploded from the moment they touched. She was flying, no, she was being carried, whisked in through the door, flattened against the wall beside the bed while she pressed herself against him. Feeling his desire, squashing herself into him while he plundered her mouth and her throat and down in the valley between her breasts and she ran her fingers urgently though the thickness of his short hair and backwards to cup his strong neck.

Her shirt seemed to float away beneath his fingers, and her own scrambling left his chest bare to her lips as she skimmed the hard planes she'd correctly dreamed lay beneath his shirt.

One bra strap slid over her shoulder as he smoothed the skin down her upper arm reverently and then the other followed, the lacy cups of her bra suspended with the impending descent something neither she nor Angus doubted. His questing hand pushed the lace aside and cupped her breast. He sighed, gazed into her eyes and then bent his head to worship her with his mouth.

Her head fell back. Exquisite. Unbearable. Undeniable. 'Please…'

He lifted his eyes to hers and her breast slipped free. They both looked at the pinkness he'd left, a mark of their mutual lust, and her belly clutched at the sensation as she savoured the heat. 'Please…?' he questioned. 'Was that more? Or was that stop…?'

He knew she didn't know and didn't wait for the answer she couldn't give. Just kissed her as if the world would end and this would be the last moment. And she flew with him to the light and the earth shifted again.

When next her eyes opened they were on the bed with her raised above him, both naked, and he held her shoulders so she leant above him. Her breasts fell as if magnetised towards his beautiful chest, so chiselled and muscular with a few sexy tendrils of hair at his throat and a low trail that led below his flat belly and the triangle of his manhood. He was so beautiful and the way he looked at her made her feel like a nymph; a hungry, insatiable, very fortunate nymph with a hand that itched to trail across his flat stomach and follow that line of hair all the way down.

Her lips ached for the feel of his mouth against hers and she leant down and allowed her nymph full rein to drink from the well that was Angus until he flipped them both over and reared above her.

'You drive me insane.'

'Good,' she said.

His hands slid down her wrists and along her elbows until she was captured beneath him. Ready, supplicating, aching for him.

'Are you sure?' he asked, and she knew the words had come hard.

'At least once in my lifetime,' she said. 'My wish…'

His eyes burned. 'Is my command.' And he eased into her.

What followed curled her toes. When she woke later, she knew the memory would stir coals of heat at inopportune times to come and that thought brought a smile, a knowing, satisfied woman's smile, to her face now that the secret had been revealed. It was true.

She turned her face to Angus's next to her in the huge four-poster bed.

'Are you okay?' he questioned.

'Mmm. Thank you.' And she grinned at him. 'Wow. Can we do that again?'

'No.' But his darkened, bedroom eyes said otherwise.

Finally she could read a little of what he felt and she couldn't help the smug little thrill it gave her to have affected him so obviously. She sighed, but it was a blissful sigh, and she felt like getting up and dancing slowly around the room in a relaxed fairy haze because the magic lingered so strongly between them.

He clarified, 'Not if we want to catch the helicopter and be back tonight.'

'Yeah, shame about that. Don't suppose we could stay.'

His eyes stopped smiling. 'I leave on Sunday.'

The fairy music froze in her head. Of course he was. He'd made sure she understood that before… And to think she'd begun to think he'd consider a change.

She looked away. She was a fool, but right at this moment she couldn't regret what had passed between them. He'd warned her. 'So, tea?'

'Tea, and then the car will be here.'

'Back to the bush.'

He'd seen her withdrawal and it was as it needed to be. He was going. Definitely. But it was going to be harder now that he'd slept with her, not easier. So much for erasing her hold on him with consummation. It would be a hundred times worse now to look back on what he had left behind. But that was life in disaster zones.

'Could you ever live at the lake again?' She didn't meet his eyes as she asked.

He couldn't look at her and not take her, so he glanced at the clock. 'Not a lot of call for disaster management.'

'You could be a GP like your father. Take over the residence practice. Retire to tranquillity.'

He could see she didn't believe that was him. He didn't either, and he guessed they both knew it. But there was a corner of his brain that found the concept alluring in its promise of peace. The corner he had to fight with. Maybe with Mia beside him.

Leave large-scale loss and the horrific memories behind for the peace and healing at Lyrebird Lake. Now he remembered the myth. See the lyrebird and be healed.

No. He wasn't the settling-down type of guy. But

it was a shame and he was glad she'd seen the inescapable truth too. Really glad.

Conversation was necessarily sparse in the noisy helicopter on the way home and not much better after they landed.

When they returned to the lake, Mia went home to the residence and Paul and Angus took off again in the helicopter.

Mia watched it go and it symbolised her brief affair with Angus. Soon he would disappear into the distance too.

Did she regret what had happened between them or was the fact that it had been inevitable an excuse? She looked around and tried to decide where to go. What to do. She had no idea what to do with herself because her brain and her emotions were all over the place.

Five minutes after they flew away the residence phone rang and gave her purpose once more.

CHAPTER SEVEN

'MIA? It's Josephine. Have Paul and Angus left yet?'

'Just gone.' Mia glanced at the clock. Angus had said they'd be about an hour. 'You okay?'

'I think I'm in labour, but I'll be fine.' The strain in Jo's voice was faint but unmistakable.

Mia chewed her lip as she thought. 'How about I come over till Paul lands? I could run you through some quiet birth practice and keep you company. If you're still in early labour when Paul returns, I can come back home for a while.' Jo didn't answer and Mia prompted, 'I'm not doing anything.'

Josephine sighed. 'That would be great. Thanks.'

Mia slipped her birth kit into the car. She'd opted to drive instead of walk the twenty minutes to Jo and Paul's house because she'd detected more trepidation than seemed appropriate in Jo's voice, and when she arrived she could see why.

Josephine was contracting strongly and a crease

of worry indented her forehead as she opened the door. 'Did Angus say how long they'd be?'

'About an hour.' Mia followed her into the house and into the kitchen. 'So how far apart are the contractions, Jo?'

'Down to two minutes,' Jo whispered, as she leant on the kitchen bench and began to breathe through another pain.

Mia glanced at the clock. 'And lasting over a minute, too. You're doing well with your breathing, Jo. Keep focussed. In through your nose, pushing your tummy out, and out through your mouth.'

The contraction finished and Josephine straightened and sighed to release the tension in her shoulders. 'The pains are much stronger than I expected. I'm glad you're here.' Her eyes filled with tears. 'Paul was supposed to set the little pool up for the birth.'

'I can do that. No problem. Everything's fine.'

'Can't we contact them?' Josephine peered out the window as if she'd see the helicopter in the sky.

'I don't think so,' Mia said, 'but they're due back in about forty-five minutes. I don't like to ring Angus's mobile in case it causes interference with the navigation instruments. I'm not sure who to ring to contact the base.'

'Men!' Josephine closed her eyes. 'Why did they have to play at flying now?'

Mia patted her shoulder. 'They'll be in trouble when

they come back. I left a big red note on the residence door so they should see that as soon as they land.'

Josephine laughed unsteadily. 'Our baby will just have to wait, then.'

Mia held up the Doppler. 'How about I check you and take your blood pressure and then we can listen to your baby?'

'Of course.' Jo rested back on the settee and Mia checked her vital signs before she lifted the bright sarong Jo was wearing and palpated her shiny round belly.

'Your baby's head's well down, turned to the right and all prepared for lift-off.' Mia smiled as she rested the hand-held foetal heart Doppler over the spot where she felt the baby's back.

The rhythmic clop, clop of Jo's baby's heartbeat filled the living room. Mia nodded. 'And he or she is happy in there, despite the walls moving.'

Jo rubbed her belly as she pulled down the sarong again. 'It must be strange for a baby to have his or her head squashed during birth.'

Mia put the hand-held device onto the coffee table for later. 'I'd imagine it is. But the thing is that babies born by Caesarean don't get squeezed and seem prone to more problems, like wet lung, when they're born than those who come through the birth canal. So nature has her reasons.'

The next pain started and Jo had no breath for talking. Mia glanced at the clock and hoped the helicopter landed soon because otherwise there was a chance Paul would miss the birth of his first child.

Jo saw her. 'He'll make it, won't he?'

'It usually takes a while to birth your first baby,' Mia said. 'I'm sure he'll be here. He'll be upset he wasn't here for the whole experience. Let's put the music on and you can go and stand in the shower.'

The men arrived half an hour later and Paul dragged Angus with him into the house like a security blanket. When he heard the Celtic Crossover music Paul's eyes widened as he realised how far along they were.

'Angus drove me,' he said unnecessarily as his head swivelled. 'Where is she?'

'In the bathroom. Go knock on the door, Paul. She'll be glad to see you. I'll sort the pool.'

She looked at Angus, who stood tall and solid in the doorway, and she wanted him to stay with her, share this, and understand the woman inside her who needed to do this job and be with birthing women.

'You want a hand?' Angus looked at the clear-sided child's pool half-inflated in the middle of the living-room floor, then at Mia's red cheeks, and she could see the amused twinkle in his eyes. 'So mid-wives require good lung capacity?'

She smiled. 'They do if the parents forget to buy a pump.'

'Paul probably expected to borrow one from the mine.' Angus nudged her out of the way. 'Here, let me do that before I leave.'

Mia's breath whooshed in relief. 'I won't say no. Thanks.' Mia busied herself with the tubing Paul had remembered, thank goodness, to connect the bath through to the tap over the kitchen sink, and then began to arrange her own gear in the corner.

'Your needs look simple,' Angus said between breaths, and she grinned at him as his face reddened.

'I'm a simple girl.' Angus blew again and Mia was glad she didn't have to inflate it all by herself. 'Fun, isn't it?'

'Oh, yeah.' They smiled at each other and suddenly the rapport from Brisbane was back and they both looked pretty happy about it, Mia realised. Maybe she'd imagined his coolness after they'd left the hotel. Maybe he wouldn't find it as easy to leave the lake as he'd thought. She was dreaming, but she could do that until she was used to the idea that he would go.

She watched his eyes begin to cross as he stared at the bung, daring the pool to leak air. Finally Angus exhaled a huge breath to finish off the pool and jammed the bung in with only a little loss of inflation.

Mia suddenly realised that this usually serious man was learning to be part of a community again, caught up in a mad moment he'd been dragged into, and Mia's shoulders began to shake with silent giggles. 'You looked so funny,' she whispered when she could talk, and glanced at the closed bathroom door as she struggled for professional composure.

Angus flopped back onto the lounge as if all his strength was gone with his breath. Mia mimed clapping her hands, careful that the two in the bathroom couldn't hear.

'My hero,' she said. My hero, she echoed the words in her mind and then pushed the thought away. 'You can come again when I have another pool to inflate.'

'Oh, goody.' He rubbed his forehead and glanced at the door too. 'So how is Jo?'

'Very calm,' Mia said, 'and she'll be even better now Paul is here.'

'Paul's pretty nervous.' Angus looked at her as if not sure how she would take the next bit. 'He asked me to hang around and I didn't like to say no. If it's okay with you, I thought I'd just sit on the veranda in case you want me.'

Mia smiled as she inserted the hose into the side of the pool and began to run warm water into it. 'I'm sure everything will be fine, Angus, but I have no problem with anything that makes the parents feel comfortable. I want their birth experience to be the best it possibly can be.'

His face was serious but, then, when was it not? 'I know that, Mia. You're pretty wonderful and they're lucky to have you as their midwife.'

'If you say so.' Praise always made her uncomfortable. She looked down at the water streaming in through the hose over the side of the pool and hoped it didn't spill out onto Jo's carpet. 'Can you watch this doesn't fall out or overflow while I check my gear, please?'

He stepped closer to the hose. 'Sure. You can show me what's on a home-birth midwife's equipment list.'

She frowned at him and then realised he was teasing her. 'The same as on a hospital midwife's list, just a bit more disposable.'

She finished setting up as the bathroom door opened and Jo looked with relief to the already half-filled pool.

'Thanks so much, Mia. We thought we'd have hours to do this, but I think this is moving along quite fast. It would be heaven to soak in the bath.'

'Angus helped me inflate it. I'm glad you're feeling that way. It's because you're moving about. When you're relaxed you allow your body to do its job. Everything is faster when you let it happen.' She looked at her face. 'How do you feel after your shower?'

Mia could see Jo literally drooped as she walked in. 'Strangely tired,' Jo said softly.

Mia held up the Doppler for non-verbal permission, and when Jo nodded she parted Jo's sarong and placed the Doppler so that the baby's heartbeats filled the room. 'Baby's happy.'

'I just said to Paul that maybe I should do this tomorrow, because I think I'm too sleepy to do it now.'

'I love it when labouring women say that.' Mia nodded. 'The hormones of labour make you feel like that, especially the endorphins. It's a part of the journey to have that feeling of sleepiness because it keeps you relaxed and able to doze between the pains. Everything is soft and stretchy and droopy and ready for the baby to do its thing, even your emotions are dulled.'

Jo sighed again. 'No wonder people forget about

labour if they feel like this, but how will I wake up enough to do the work when I have to?'

Mia smiled. 'Women often say that. You will. Trust me, and especially trust your body to know what it's doing.'

Paul looked at Mia. 'Jo and I were talking and we wondered if you'd mind if we make a video so Jo can see what happened. In case she gets a bit vague on what happens later.'

'Of course not,' Mia said. 'Birth videos are so special and beautiful. But you'll need another person because you or I can't do two jobs, Paul. Your job is to be there every minute for Jo as she needs you.'

'We thought about it before, but didn't know who to ask, but we've sorted that out now.' Paul looked sheepishly at the only other person in the room. 'Angus?'

Angus looked at Jo. 'If that's what you want, I'd be honoured.'

'Good,' Jo said, and smiled until her breath caught and she leant heavily against Paul as the next contraction started. 'I need to get back under some water.' She looked longingly at the bath.

Mia nodded and reached for the Doppler. 'Can I listen again through this contraction and a minute after, if that's OK? That way we know that baby's heart rate doesn't slow after the contraction. Then I can leave you to really enjoy those first moments of weightlessness.'

'Sure.' Jo said the word as she exhaled and they all breathed with her. Even Angus.

After that, when Jo lay back in the bath, she sighed in a big relieved whoosh and they could all see the respite the water gave her. Her head rested against the side of the pool and the heat pinked her cheeks as she stretched her arms and legs and revelled in the buoyancy. 'Oh, my.' She leaned back more on the inflated sides of the pool and closed her eyes, and the water lapped over her breasts and the rounded dome of her belly.

She drifted gently from side to side and breathed slowly through the next pain like a contented puppy.

The birth, when it happened, was everything Jo and Paul had dreamt of and what Mia had wanted Angus to see.

Paul had not long slipped into the pool so Jo could lean back against his chest and she squatted easily as the water held her weight. Their baby emerged under the water within the next hour, first his downy hair, then his face and chin, into his mother's hands, videoed by Angus from the edge of the pool.

The body was born in a smooth arc and Mia reached in and lifted him from the water so that he felt the first touch of air with his mouth free and then he rested against his mother's chest and blinked.

Angus captured the incredible ambience of the room, the soft music, the murmurs of encouragement from Mia, the gasp of amazement of Paul, and then those precious first unfocussed stares from the baby's dark blue eyes as he gazed up at his parents for the first time.

With barely a whimper Paul and Jo's baby adapted to extra-uterine life quietly as he lay against his mother's breasts. His lower body floated in the water as he stared around, and Mia slipped a little cap on his head to keep him warm.

Later, when the cord had stopped pulsating, Paul cut it, and didn't faint, which he'd threatened to do, and after the placenta had been delivered Mia helped Jo from the bath so mother and baby could slip into the shower together.

Afterwards Paul took his son from Jo's hands and clumsily dressed him with Angus's encouragement. Mia surprised a look of such longing on Angus's face that she felt tears prick her eyes. He'd missed out on this moment, had never felt what Paul was feeling now, and maybe never would. But the future was his choice.

Angus glanced across at her and his face closed when he saw that she'd understood. Mia felt the loss of that communication like a blow to her heart.

Mia checked that all was well with Jo, made cups of tea, chased the three of them back to rest in their bedroom and left them to be a family so there was only her and Angus left.

They moved to the veranda of Jo's house and drank their own tea.

'Wow,' Angus said under his breath, but she heard him.

'Still stunned by the beauty of the birth?' she said.

Angus looked at her. 'That was an amazing experience, and nothing like any of the births I saw during my training. No wonder you love what you do.'

Good. He could see what it should be. She remembered the unobtrusiveness of Angus's filming. He'd barely been there, so sensitive to ensure he didn't impinge on Jo's birthing space, drifting around the edges of the room, and even from Mia's own observations she could tell he'd concentrated mainly on faces and ambience. It would be a beautiful reminder for Jo and Paul.

'You can imagine why women love water births,' she said, 'because they feel so light, can shift position without effort, and the expanse of water around them makes them feel protected but not exposed, like a woman can feel exposed on a bed in a labour ward.'

He shook his head in wonder. 'Jo looked so peaceful and in control.'

'That's right. She was. It was her birth and she got what she asked for and nothing else.' Mia sighed and relaxed back against the bench she sat on and drank in the glory of the early evening. She sipped her herbal tea and went over the labour's progression in her mind.

'Everything went smoothly,' she said, 'as it normally does, but it's always rewarding to look back and review the events.'

Angus glanced across at her. 'I noticed you didn't put your hands in the water much. Is there a reason?'

Mia nodded. 'The less other people's hands are in the water the better. It's warm water, quite capable of growing bugs, so the least amount of contamination from others, the better for mother and baby.'

He rubbed his neck and she admired the way he was non-judgementally resolving the issues he'd thought he would have. 'What about the cord around the neck? How do you check it isn't tight?'

Good question, she thought. 'I don't check it. Baby will come out and if there is an unexpected delay then I'd get Mum to stand up so I could see what the hold-up was. The whole idea is for as little interference as possible. When the head is born, excessive touching has the slim possibility of making the baby breathe too early.'

Angus frowned. 'Have you ever seen a baby breathe under the water unexpectedly?'

She smiled at him. 'No.' He was certainly engaged. 'These are all the questions the parents ask. I'm glad you're asking them too.'

Angus looked into the distance across the lake. 'What you do is fascinating stuff. I'd like to know more about it because I didn't realise I knew so little.'

'Okay.' Mia nodded. 'Obviously baby is still connected to mum via the umbilical cord and still getting oxygen. The baby isn't in a hurry for oxygen and isn't stimulated to breathe until it hits the impact of the air out of the water. So a little time fully submerged straight after birth is okay as long as when a baby is lifted out of the water you do so in a smooth motion—as a midwife I usually do that bit—and his or her head is never put back under the water again at that stage. Just onto Mum's chest if the cord is long enough.'

She'd done that in there. Angus nodded. 'What about if the baby is distressed?'

Mia shook her head. 'Water birth is a choice, not a prison sentence.' There was no doubt in her voice and he saw the responsible practitioner he might have doubted before today.

'Circumstances change,' she said. 'A distressed baby has no place in a water birth. That's why I listen with the Doppler.'

'If there was meconium-stained amniotic fluid,' he wondered out loud, 'then that's a contra-indication as well.'

'Absolutely,' she said. 'That baby may have been distressed at some stage, may have gasped inside the uterus already, and it can't be guaranteed he won't come out gasping. So if suddenly her water breaks and that amniotic fluid has a green tinge, she has to get out.'

Angus nodded. 'Is that a problem? Getting someone to move?'

Mia shook her head vehemently. 'Not if I've explained beforehand that the only reason I would ask was if I had a concern about the baby.'

'Of course,' he said. It all made sense. 'I can see

that a mother would be extremely motivated to move in that case.'

'And she hasn't had drugs that have dulled her common sense. Home birth has so much to offer for those who are comfortable with it.' She grinned up at him. 'And the stats are extremely good if you compare them to the complications that happen in hospitals.'

'Not Lyrebird Lake Hospital, though,' he teased, and she laughed and he loved the way her eyes crinkled when she did that. Another memory to store away for when he left.

'No,' she said, and he could hear the pride in her voice. Such pride when she'd only been here weeks. This place really did capture people. She went on, 'The lake has fabulous statistics because our births are pretty similar to having a birth at home anyway.'

He was adjusting his way of thinking and he could see the idea of that excited her. It seemed strange to him that she could be so enmeshed in the future of his home town hospital when he wasn't. 'How long has the midwifery aspect been going on here?' he asked.

She sat up straighter. 'Montana's been here a little over two years. Her first husband died soon after she conceived Dawn, and Andy brought her here to help her over the loss when Dawn was born.'

'So Dawn's not Andy's baby?' he said, and he found himself wondering about Simon and his relationship with his stepfather.

'She may as well be. Andy found them on the

mountain the day she was born, and he's been like a dad to her since then.'

Angus's could feel shock course through him. No doubt his eyebrows had nearly disappeared into his hairline, but that was way too much. 'Montana had her baby on a mountain?'

Mia shrugged with a little too much nonchalance. 'Quick labours happen sometimes. She was a couple of weeks early and Montana was on her way to the hospital but ran out of time. She had her baby on an escarpment at daybreak, by herself.'

'Hence the name Dawn.' He shuddered at the thought, but then remembered the peace of the birth he'd just witnessed and guessed Montana would have had the same faith that Mia obviously had in a woman's natural ability to give birth.

These women were incredible.

Maybe if he could understand her friends he could understand Mia and why she affected him so much. 'So what's Misty's story?'

'Misty found Ben almost drowned.' Mia decided to avoid the fact that Misty had seen Ben's danger in a vision. Angus was having enough trouble getting used to natural birth.

She went on, 'Misty resuscitated him and took him home to recover, and after she left Ben followed her here. Tammy is Ben's teenage daughter from his first marriage and Misty helped Ben and Tammy become closer before Tammy's baby was born.'

Angus looked confused and she smiled. 'The baby your father was visiting the day you arrived.'

He nodded. 'You're all like a big family.'

Her voice softened. 'Yes, we are. Though there's always room for others in the family.' She silently added, a family he could be a part of if he wanted, but she hoped he'd get it.

He didn't comment so she continued, but couldn't help her disappointment. 'I'm glad I came here. I love the work and this is a great place to bring up my child. I don't have any other family except my friends so being here with them is perfect.'

He nodded. 'I can understand that.' He looked at her. 'I just can't join it.' So he had heard what she'd left unsaid.

She sucked air in and let it out. Then she smiled at him. 'I'm sad for you, but everyone has their own journey, Angus. I understand that.' She stood up. 'I'll just go and check the new family and help Paul clean up. I'll see you back at the residence.'

CHAPTER EIGHT

THE next morning Simon appeared at Angus's elbow and he thought again how much Simon looked like his mother. Funny how that thought didn't bother him when a week ago he could have cheerfully strangled her.

'So what did you do as a kid around here, Dad?' Simon appeared dressed to accompany him on his morning walk, and Angus shifted over on the path to make room. Angus looked down at his son and then back along the memories of childhood as Simon fell into step beside him.

'Mostly I walked or swam. Neither of which required company,' he said dryly. 'I was pretty solitary even then.'

Simon increased his pace to keep up. 'What about for excitement?'

'Oh. Excitement?' Angus thought of the amazing birth he'd witnessed yesterday. That had been pretty exciting. But twenty years ago he hadn't attended too many births.

'In Lyrebird Lake?' Angus smiled. 'Except for your mother…' crikey, he could even joke about her now, this was unbelievable '…the only exciting thing I found to do was exploring the gold mines and old cradle washing sites in the creek. I was into geology and gold panning in those days.'

He stared off into the distance. 'Used to have an old map that outlined the tunnel claims. I'd spend hours down the mines, which your grandfather didn't know about. The map's probably still buried somewhere in the house, along with my caving gear.'

Simon's eyes had lit up. 'So there's still gold mines here and shafts and tunnels?'

Angus frowned. 'They boarded most of them up when one of the younger children fell into a disused shaft. I remember the day they found her, but it was too late.' He thought about that. 'Probably that's why I was attracted to the job I do now.'

Simon nodded impatiently for the rest of the story. 'When they shut the mines, did that stop you exploring?'

'No,' he said reluctantly. 'Just made it more illicit.' He looked at the intensity in his son's grey eyes and shuddered at the thought of Simon crawling through some of the places he'd crawled through. 'But now I've spent too much of my life digging people out of rubble to be comfortable for you to try. I'm not keen on finding the map for you.'

Simon's shoulders drooped and Angus restrained from adding anything else in case he encouraged his son more.

After a moment of silence Simon changed the subject. 'This is a pretty sleepy town, isn't it?'

Angus looked along the deserted path beside the lake and regretted the last few minutes' conversation. He felt like slapping his forehead at his own stupidity. Nineteen-year-olds didn't get diverted, but Angus let the conversation lie. They wouldn't be here much longer and the less said about mine shafts the better.

'Sleepy can be a good thing.'

'Hmm.' Simon didn't sound convinced. 'Here comes Mia. What happened to her hair? I liked it the other way.' Simon shook his head at the strangeness of women. 'I think she likes you, Dad.'

'Hmmm,' Angus said in return, and watched his nemesis approach from the hospital. He agreed with Simon about her hair, but the fact that she'd wanted to change it and had was all part of the intoxicating package that was Mia.

He couldn't help his body's response to her, the leap in his pulse, the kick in his gut, but he could do without it, would have to do without it. She wasn't leaving the lake for a fling and he wasn't staying. He had places to go and people to save, and Mia deserved someone who would always be there for her.

He glanced at the mischief in Simon's eyes and clarified before she was in earshot. 'I'm leaving the day after tomorrow.'

Simon raised his eyebrows. 'Why?' Simon smiled at the two women. 'I wonder who the honey is with the pram?' he whispered to his father.

Angus hoped he'd heard him wrong.

Mia came up and she looked more at Simon than at Angus. 'Hello, people.' Mia indicated the pretty blonde-haired woman. 'This is Emma. Emma's our first home-grown bachelor of midwifery student, and this is her daughter, Grace. Grace is two and the first baby to be actually born in Lyrebird Lake for a long time.'

Emma smiled. 'I was lucky Montana was there for me.'

Mia smiled and gestured to Angus without meeting his eyes. 'This is Angus, Dr Ned's son, and his son, Simon. Angus was with me when Jo and Paul had their baby yesterday.'

Emma nodded. 'Wow. Paul said Jo is so thrilled. Was the birth awesome?'

Angus smiled. 'It was.'

Mia looked at Simon, though she directed the question at Angus. 'Have you plans for today, Angus?' He frowned and tried to pinpoint the feeling Mia asked under protest and he wondered who'd set her the task.

He fished. 'No, why?'

Mia nodded, perhaps fatalistically he thought, as

if she'd expected to be disappointed. Obviously he'd given the wrong answer.

'You and Simon have been invited to a barbecue at Misty and Ben Moore's house on the lake this afternoon. Ned and Louisa are going as well. And Emma and Tammy will be there so that's two young people for Simon. It's sort of an impromptu pre-wedding party Misty and Montana have organised.'

Angus suppressed a sigh. Company. A party. Oh, joy. He felt less like socialising with a group of people he barely knew than walking over hot coals, but he owed it to his father to at least try. His father never stopped saying how Andy and Ben had been good to him. Somebody had needed to be, seeing as how he himself had never come back.

He wasn't sure how to deal with that guilt and he supposed smilingly at some party was probably a good place to start.

As if he'd read his father's reluctance, Simon piped up with the clincher. 'Are you going too, Mia?'

'I'll be there.' Mia looked less than thrilled, but Angus had the feeling she would have been happier if he wasn't going. The sooner he left this town the better for both of them.

'Two o'clock,' she said, and left them to their walk.

'Bye, Simon, bye, Angus,' Emma said as she followed Mia, and he was sure Simon smiled more widely than was needed as she walked away.

Angus couldn't help the curtness in his voice.

'You know you're too young to be attracted to women with babies. You've got your life to live.'

Simon raised his eyebrows. 'Like you did? Was being childless and free better for you when you were my age?' Simon looked at him with wisdom beyond his years and shook his head. 'Did Mum do the right thing when she didn't tell you about me?'

Angus felt the pain slice into him. The same pain he'd felt when Simon's mother had told him she'd miscarried. The pain that said he was fooling himself if he thought he could just pick up after twenty years and advise his son on his life. He sighed. 'No. She didn't do the right thing. She had no right to lie and exclude me from your childhood and your life, and I will never forgive her.'

Simon looked him up and down and Angus felt sadly wanting. 'That's your problem, Angus.' Simon called him by name deliberately. 'Not mine. My stepfather was a good dad, and he treated me no differently than my sisters.' Simon looked at him. 'My mother did what she thought she had to do. Don't disrespect my mother.'

He was silent and Angus didn't know what to say not to make it worse.

Simon looked at him once more, but Angus couldn't read what his son was thinking. 'I would like to get to know you,' Simon said, 'but don't think you can tell me how to run my life because you don't have the right.' And he spun on his heel and walked back towards the residence.

Angus watched him go and rubbed the back of his neck. He wished he could retrieve the words he'd rashly spoken to his son, but it was too late now. He shook his head and walked on. Full marks to Simon for loyalty to his mother. She had been young and no doubt it wouldn't have been easy with him in the early years if they'd stayed together. He wanted out of here. His father's wedding couldn't come quickly enough.

That afternoon, in her room, Mia finished her make-up for the party and was about to leave for Misty's when she heard the phone ring.

Ned and Louisa had already left and Mia had no idea where Angus had gone. He'd been almost taciturn after his walk and she'd steered clear of him. She dashed into the hallway and picked up the phone.

'Mia. It's Simon.'

Of course it was for Angus, she thought with a sigh, and she didn't know where he was. 'Oh, hi, Simon. Do you want your dad?'

'Ah, no.' There was silence on the other end of the phone and Mia frowned.

'You okay?' She kept her voice light.

'Actually, I need a favour.' A hesitant Simon seemed out of character and the back of Mia's neck prickled.

'Are you in trouble?'

Simon hesitated, then… 'Sort of.'

Mia frowned. 'Spit it out, Simon, I'm getting worried here.'

'I'm sort of stuck in a mine shaft…' She heard the nonchalance that didn't quite come off in Simon's voice.

Mia's other hand came to hold the phone so that her arms crossed over her heart. It's okay, she told herself, he's still talking, he doesn't sound hurt.

'What sort of stuck, Simon? Do we need a tow truck, an ambulance or just me to pick you up?'

'Just you.' The relief was evident in his voice. There was a pause and then he said, 'I love you for understanding, Mia.'

Mia frowned. 'I love you too, Simon, but now I'm really scared. I'm getting your father.'

'No. He'll think I'm a fool. He'd never get stuck. I don't know. Can't you just come and lift the board off me so I can crawl out?'

Mia jammed the phone under her chin and dug in her pocket for her mobile phone. She had no idea where Angus was, but she needed to contact him right now. 'Where are you, Simon?'

'Dad and I had words this morning. I was angry and he probably still is too.'

She thought of Angus and what she knew of him. 'Not that angry. Where are you?'

She heard Simon sigh. 'I walked down past the end of the lake on the path and then straight up the hill along a gully. The outside of the mine had a steel grate on it, but the lock was broken. I'm only just inside the entrance.'

She frowned. 'You didn't break it, did you, Simon?'

'No.' He sounded genuinely horrified and Mia sighed back against the wall. Then others had been in there too, so hopefully it wasn't too bad.

'Give me five minutes and I'll ring you back and tell you where I am. *Don't move.*'

She searched her mobile for the number Angus had given her and rang him. He answered on the second ring.

'Angus! Where are you?'

'Mia? Just coming up the front path.'

'Wonderful.' She disconnected and headed to the front of the house.

'Nice phone call,' he said when she opened the door, but at the look on Mia's face his gaze sharpened.

'Simon needs you. Follow me.'

Angus put his hand on her shoulder. He was very quick for a big man, because she'd turned and started walking as she spoke. 'Hang on a minute. Where is my son?' he said.

Mia looked at his hand preventing her from moving on and raised her eyebrows. Angus stepped back.

'Simon has trapped himself in the entrance to a mine up the gully past the lake.'

Angus had his gaze fixed on her face. 'Which mine?'

Which mine? That didn't sound good. 'How many are there?' Mia asked.

'About twenty.'

Mia sagged against the wall. 'I don't think he

knows, but he rang the house phone so he has his mobile and there's enough service to make the call.'

'Probably one of the higher ones, then.' Angus pulled his phone from his pocket and punched in Simon's number.

'Simon?' He listened. 'Yes, she had to tell me. It's okay. I need to know which mine. We'll drive to the end of the lake and walk up the gully, but is it one that faces the lake or one that faces the mountains?'

Simon must have told him because he snapped his phone shut and reached for his keys in his pocket. 'You want to come?'

No doubt he had a use for her or she wouldn't have been invited. 'Yes, please.'

'Thank you,' he said. 'You shouldn't play in mine shafts without a second person.'

'I knew I had a use,' she said.

He smiled inside as they climbed into the car. She had uses all right. No doubt she could become essential to pretty much everything in his life if he let her. But he wasn't going there. Right now Simon was his main priority and he needed to be sure they were all safe.

As they drove into the car park at the end of the lake Mia said, 'Simon said you two had words this morning.'

Straight-to-the-point Mia. Would he miss that aspect of her? Probably. Angus sighed. Another sigh. He seemed to be doing a lot of that this week. With his father and the awkwardness between them, with Simon and his gaffe that morning, and now with Mia. Lyrebird Lake was nothing if not emotionally exhausting. Pretty hard for a guy who didn't do emotion.

'Yes, we did have words,' Angus said. 'Simon stood up for his mother as a son should, and I vented when I shouldn't have. But I only want what's best for him too.'

'The fact that you care is more important than the teething problems the two of you will have while you find your relationship.'

He looked at her. 'Thank you. You're right and I'll just have to trust that Simon will see that too. Now, let's go find him.'

In the end it wasn't far to walk. Simon was sitting just inside the shaft entrance where a small beam had landed awkwardly against his leg and pinned him. His face was dirty, but he didn't seem to be injured.

Angus pulled the grate back and examined the other beam that was holding the door then slid past it to stand in the shaft. 'Simon.' He nodded.

Simon nodded back. 'Dad. Sorry you had to come out.'

'No problem. Bad luck it had to catch you.'

Mia looked from one to the other and shook her head. Men. 'Does it hurt?'

Simon looked immeasurably relieved his father didn't seem angry. 'No.' He grinned at Mia. 'Horribly embarrassing though.'

Angus laughed and crouched down next to him. 'Really bad luck.' Then the humour dropped out of his voice. 'But it could have been a lot worse. Let's get you out of here.'

The beam was heavy and there was no way Mia would have been able to lift it without Angus. She helped Simon slide out from underneath it as Angus lifted, and the creaking from the roof had them all scuttling out as soon as possible.

Before they left, Angus pulled a spare padlock from his glove compartment and re-clipped the grill.

Simon looked worried. 'They won't have a key.'

'The owners can cut the lock off if they want. What they won't want is other people stuck in there.'

Simon looked away and Mia could see the tide of colour on his neck.

'I'm not saying I never got stuck,' Angus said, and Mia saw Simon relax back in the seat. Well done, Angus, Mia applauded, and she smiled to herself. They'd be fine. Just needed to sort out the dynamics and they'd be better without her eavesdropping.

The drive back to the house was accomplished with little conversation and already they were late for the barbecue. 'I'll go ahead and tell them you're both on your way.' She smiled at Simon. 'Won't be mentioning the side trip.'

'Thanks, Mia.' He looked at his father. 'And for calling Dad.'

'No problem. See you both soon at Misty's house.'

* * *

Angus stood at the edge of the garden and encouraged Simon to pass in front of him while he hesitated to watch the festivities for a moment.

The white-timbered house was clearly a new two-storey and the large veranda on top would give sweeping views over the lake. He liked the wide, straight stairway that joined the top floor to the grass below and the white latticework that scallop-laced the edges underneath.

Everyone was downstairs on the grass and the branches of a huge gumtree at the edge of the yard blocked the direct rays of the sun from the party. A cool afternoon zephyr drifted off the lake, making the temperature pleasant.

There were only three couples and two younger women with babies, but it seemed a crowd to him.

One of the young mums would be Ben's daughter, Tammy, whom Mia had mentioned, and the other was Emma, whom they'd met that morning.

Ned had his arm around Louisa's waist and looked the most relaxed he'd seen him since he'd arrived as he stood with a can of beer in his hand and hailed Simon. It was actually great to see his dad so happy.

Typically, Angus's radar zeroed in on Mia at the other side of the garden next to two other couples, and she turned and gestured for him to meet them.

He crossed to her side and he wasn't quite sure how, but the easy space they made for him seemed to strip his usual aloofness at gatherings.

His eyes met and locked for a moment with Mia's, and when she smiled across at him suddenly it wasn't so bad. 'This is Ned's son, Angus. This is Montana and Andy.' A wave of her hand. 'And Misty and Ben.'

So these were the doctors who had helped his father keep Lyrebird Lake Hospital going. The men shook hands easily and he saw that both were laconic and relaxed, and his own tension began to slip away.

'Paul and Josephine say you fly.' Andy smiled at him.

Angus nodded. 'News gets around.'

'How unusual for a country town.' Andy grinned with gentle sarcasm and Angus liked the guy for his easy friendship. This wasn't too bad.

'I doubt it's changed since you were a kid here,' Andy went on. 'Anyway, I've a light plane myself, two-seater Cessna, though Montana's not keen on it.' Andy glanced at his wife and the look that passed between the couple made Angus realise that there was a lot he didn't know about happiness and contentment.

He couldn't help a quick look at Mia to see if she'd seen it too, but she was listening to a dark-haired toddler as if the little girl held the secrets of the world. She was absorbed in the toddler's story and her attention showed how much she loved kids.

He looked back at Andy. 'Mia coped very well with the helicopter yesterday.'

Andy nodded. 'I heard the chopper come in and go out a couple of times. So that was you?'

Angus tore his eyes away from Mia. 'I had to see some people in Brisbane and Mia came for the ride. In the afternoon Paul came up for a spin before dark.'

'He gets picked up in dark cars by men in suits,' Mia said as, still holding the little girl's hand, she drew her up to stand in front of Angus. 'This is Dawn. Montana and Andy's eldest child.'

He had no experience of serious little girls. 'Hello, Dawn,' Angus said gravely, and the little girl held out her hand. Angus wasn't sure if he was supposed to shake it or bestow a kiss. He bent and took the tiny fingers in his and gently shook them. Dawn had a blue bunny tucked under her arm and Angus shook the bunny's hand too.

'And who's this?' he asked Dawn.

'Wabbit.'

'Hello, Wabbit,' Angus said seriously, and Dawn smiled shyly up at him. He felt Mia watching him and, uncomfortable, he smiled at the little girl and then stepped back.

Mia grinned at him and he felt like he'd passed a test. But it didn't matter because he was leaving this town. He needed to remember that.

'What's with the dark cars and suits?' Ben was harking back to Mia's opening comment and the last thing Angus wanted was for them to think he was some sort of secret agent.

He shrugged it off with a joke. 'Just trying to impress Mia.'

Ben frowned. 'Why? You're leaving aren't you?'

Mia shot a look at Ben and wondered where that had come from. She supposed Misty must have mentioned Mia's confusion over Angus, but it shocked her to have Ben champion her like that.

And it had certainly stopped the conversation.

Angus met Ben's look with a cool one of his own, and shrugged. 'Mia's a big girl. It's been an interesting trip all round. But I have to get back to work.'

So she was part of his interesting time. That wiped out any hope she had of an earth-shattering change between them from yesterday's events.

Andy stepped in. 'So, no chance of you taking over the general practice while your father goes on his honeymoon?'

Mia wondered if it was more to lighten the tension than anything. Then again Andy had always been single minded about staffing Lyrebird Lake. She remembered when he'd snared Montana into coming. But in that instance he may have had ulterior motives, seeing as he'd fancied her from the start.

Angus looked away from Ben to Andy, and Mia saw the stiffness in his stance loosen. 'I'm a little out of practice for general practice, if you'll excuse the pun. Maybe another time.'

Andy nodded philosophically. 'Keep it in mind. We're always looking for new recruits, especially as your father is looking to retire, and an ex-local would be even better.'

The barbecue, the third Mia had had since she'd been at the lake, was the usual light-hearted affair, apart from the incident with Ben and Angus. The whole time, though, Mia had been aware of where Angus stood, who he was talking or not talking to, and wondering if things would have been different if they hadn't made love in Brisbane.

Which was ridiculous. She couldn't be sorry she'd slept with him. It had been an earth-shaking education, if nothing else on his side, and there was no denying the connection between them. It just wasn't his time to settle down and she had to make a place for her child.

They were two grown people making decisions on cold, hard facts, but even now she ached in a delicious way just thinking about their time together.

But there was no denying Angus would be gone after the wedding and she needed to resolve any ridiculous longings.

The problem now was how to forget what had happened. Being with Angus had rocked her with her own unexpected response. Even now she could feel the firmness of his mouth against hers and the flutter in her belly that she'd never expected.

Maybe it had nothing to do with Angus. Maybe because she was pregnant she was ripe for the plucking. Hormones and increased blood supply making her susceptible to attractive men. And his kissing. Yeah right! Find another excuse.

Soon she too would have a child like those here on the hips of their parents, but not with Angus.

How many times did she have to tell herself?

'Did you sleep with him?' Misty had steered her aside and Mia hadn't even noticed.

Her brain froze. How did Misty know? 'What?'

'You did! You just have to look at you both. Mia! Are you mad? He's leaving after tomorrow.'

'Well, at least I can't get pregnant.'

Misty shook her head. 'How can you go from being a twenty-six-year-old virgin before Mark to sleeping with a guy you've known for six days?'

Mia looked down at the grass beneath her feet. 'Six days is a long time.'

'Obviously.' Misty shook her head. 'The sparks between you two are off the scale. You'll get hurt.'

Mia lifted her head. 'I know. And I won't have that freedom of choice when my baby is born so I can't regret it. Can you understand I would have always wondered?'

Misty shook her head and the worry was in her voice. 'Not a good enough reason.'

Mia sighed. 'I think I love him.'

Misty froze and her voice softened. 'Oh, Mia. Honey. I'm sorry. It's too late.' She shook her head. 'Damn these men for having such a hold over us.'

'Damn Ben?' Mia teased, and Misty smiled.

'Well, no, but it's horrible during the in-between phase.'

'It's okay, Misty. I understand that he is going.' Mia braved a smile. 'I'll just have to catch lots of babies and forget him. My child and I will have a good life here and maybe one day it will be different.'

CHAPTER NINE

THE morning of Ned and Louisa's wedding dawned clear and bright, and Mia hated it that instead of joy for the older couple her first thought involved Angus, and that tomorrow he would be gone.

She threw back the covers and the sun shone straight in on her, a beam of golden light that rested on her rounded stomach—which she was sure just moved!

The first flutter! Was it too early? She was already eighteen weeks and it was possible. She'd been waiting so long for this and she'd nearly missed it by wallowing in Angus lust.

That's it.

She wasn't going there. Finished. Amazing interlude—memories like Thursday's birth that would never go away, but he was *unavailable.* Life went on. Now all she had to do was hold on to that concept.

She remembered her conversation with Misty the previous day and reminded herself she was still glad she'd said yes, but would move on.

* * *

When Angus drove to the church with Simon, all he could think of was he wanted this wedding over and them both gone. He didn't know how much more denial he could take.

The first person he saw—or had he subconsciously sought her out?—was Mia. Beautiful Mia, dressed in a floral sundress, her beautiful shoulders bare and just the hint of her baby showing in the roundness of her belly. Again, like the first day, she stood framed by the door, looking like an angel. She handed out programmes and warm, friendly smiles, and she slammed into his heart like he'd driven into a tree.

Her hair shone as a shining red halo around her head as it started to wave itself back to curls, and until she saw him, the curve of her lips had beckoned like a promise.

Until she saw him.

'Hello, Angus.'

He seemed to have moved from car to Mia in an instant with no memory of where he'd parked or how he'd got there.

'Mia.' He had to say it. 'You look beautiful.'

'Thank you.' She smiled impersonally, and that hurt. 'Your suit looks great. Your father is in the vestry.' Then she looked away from him to his son and grinned. The sunbeam he'd wanted for himself.

'Hello, Simon. Don't you look handsome?'

Well, what did he expect? It was good she'd decided to keep her distance. Sensible. He was leaving.

He forced himself to walk away and he ducked his head to enter the domed-shaped room at the back of the church. His father was shifting from foot to foot when he found him in the vestry and Angus shook off his own concerns.

Ned looked old and worried, but still a handsome old dog dressed in his suit. 'So that's where I get my good looks,' Angus said as he stopped beside him.

'But not your height,' his father attempted to joke, but his fingers fiddled with his tie until it looked closer to mangled than made.

'Let me fix that.' Angus straightened the knot and smoothed the silk until it bulged neatly from his father's collar. 'I'm glad I stayed for today, Dad. Congratulations on finding a wonderful woman like Louisa. I'm sure you'll both be very happy.'

Ned's faded grey eyes looked into his. 'Do you think I could make her happy?' He shook his head, obviously troubled. 'I couldn't make your mother happy.'

Angus shrugged. 'Some people are harder to keep happy than others.' The truth was simple when he thought about it. He wished he'd thought about it earlier in his life. 'Louisa loves you. That's all that matters.'

Ned peered at him with mock suspicion. 'Who are you? Where's my son?'

Angus laughed and patted Ned on the shoulder. 'I

know. I'll try more. Maybe the lyrebird has healed me,' he joked.

Ned peered at him and his faded grey eyes sparkled with delight. 'Have you seen it?'

Angus suppressed his sigh. 'I was joking, Dad. I haven't seen it. Mia said something the other day and I remembered you talking about the myth once.'

Ned raised his finger. 'Don't mock the bird, son. I saw it and all the angst from your mother fell away. It cured me. You ask Andy and Ben. They saw it too. You see the lyrebird and you'll know you've almost reached peace.'

Angus looked at him, but didn't say anything. It was his father's wedding day. He could be romantic if he wanted.

'I shouldn't push you.' His father did look less worried and that was good. 'It's just not something I expected you to say,' Ned said, 'but it's helped.'

At least he'd said something right. 'I'm glad.'

'And I'm glad you came.' Ned drew a deep breath and stood up straight. 'Now, let's get out there before I get maudlin at my own wedding.'

Louisa glowed with happiness in a cream afternoon gown straight out of a Jane Austen novel as she walked down the aisle. Her white hair framed the high neck and the gown flowed to a stately demi-train at the back with tiny pearl buttons from neck to her rounded waist.

Mia sighed mistily as Ned took her hand and they waited for the ceremony to start.

She tried not to dwell on Angus as he stood tall and straight beside his father, didn't want to see how his tailored suit accentuated his muscular thighs, or think about what it had been like to be held against his sculpted chest and stroked by those strong, tanned hands.

Instead she offered to hold Emma's toddler, who squirmed on her mother's lap, though she wondered who would gain the most comfort in the exchange.

'You sure?' Emma looked down at her daughter. 'I think Grace has a temperature and it's making her cross.' Emma smoothed her daughter's hair. 'She's been off her food too, poor lamb. I wouldn't have come, but Dr Ned and Louisa have been so good to me since my mum got sick I wanted to see the wedding.'

'Sometimes when kids aren't well they'll sit more quietly on someone else's knee. As if they expect Mum to fix them and you can't. She won't have expectations of me. Give me a go.'

Emma passed Grace across, and Mia stared into the sick-baby grey eyes below her and smiled. 'Cuddle in, sweetheart,' Mia said, and rocked her gently until her eyes closed.

Angus saw them as he stood side on to the congregation and his heart contracted. Mia with a child in her arms. He'd never seen that with his own son.

Never been there as Simon grew, fell ill, became well, learnt to do all the things a father could teach a child.

Children weren't meant to be a part of his life. He accepted that, but they were certainly a part of Mia's. Mia would find someone else. Mia would find a man who could help her parent her child. Like Simon's mother had.

It just wouldn't be him.

After the ceremony Ned and Louise floated up the aisle to the accompaniment of Andy's inexpert but extremely enthusiastic bagpipes and everyone was smiling except for Angus, who met Mia's eyes as he went past.

He saw Mia's arms tighten instinctively around the little girl in her lap.

Children were so much more important than chasing impossible dreams, Mia thought. She didn't smile, didn't feel like pretending any more that everything was fine. He was a good man, but he wasn't her man.

She watched him lift his head and look away. Mia had known it was never meant to be more than a fleeting rainbow. How ironic she was well over Mark. She needed to get over Angus now.

She dragged her mind away from impossible dreams. 'Grace is asleep and I see her pram against the wall there.' Mia wanted out. 'You know, Emma, how about I walk to the residence with Grace while the photos are taken here? Everyone will be back in half an hour and that will give you a chance to congratulate Dr Ned and Louisa and get your photo with them before you come and take her home.'

Emma looked longingly towards the wedding party. 'What about you? What if she cries?'

'She'll be fine. I'm a nurse. I'll just pop her into my bed with a sheet over her and won't leave her until you come. I think she's getting hotter. I'll take her temperature and give her some medicine to bring her temp down too.'

'I worry when Emma's sick. It's so hard to know what's normal and what's not. Mum broke my thermometer just before I came and the chemist's shut. I could ask someone to look at her in the house surgery later. Before I take her home.'

'That's a good idea. Always listen to your instincts if you don't know whether to see the doctor or not. Let's get the pram and pop her in.'

They settled the little girl and they both looked down at her curled in the pram. Emma drew a big breath and Mia could see her wavering in her decision to leave Grace's side.

'Thanks, Mia. I'll only be half an hour. It's good talking to you about this. I can't talk to Mum now that she's so sick and Dad just worries if I say there's anything wrong with Grace. I wanted to ask one of the doctors about her, but didn't like to before the wedding.'

'It must be hard, being a single mum,' Mia squeezed her arm. 'I'll know how you feel when my baby arrives.'

Emma grinned as she thought about Mia's baby. She lifted a thin sheet over her daughter in her pram. 'Montana will be back at work by then, but you'll still be off on maternity leave when Misty goes off. I'd better study hard for those shifts coming up.'

'You'll be a great midwife and, who knows, maybe Grace will grow up to be one too.'

Emma grinned. 'And your daughter, too, if it's a girl.' They both smiled.

Emma turned reluctantly to follow the wedding party. 'Thanks for this. I won't be long. As soon as the official photos are done, I'll come.'

Mia shooed her. 'Don't worry, we'll be fine.'

Ten minutes later Mia was thinking, famous last words. Even as she pushed the pram up the front path of the residence Grace seemed to be redder in the face and dots of perspiration dotted her downy cheeks.

Mia had picked up the pace and turned the pram so the cool breeze had streamed over Grace's body and cooled her, but the little girl obviously had some virus. Convulsions could happen, even when children were slightly febrile, and Grace was more than that.

Mia didn't need to call anyone yet, but she wouldn't hesitate to call Angus if she was worried. It didn't occur to her to call Ben or Andy, which, if she'd thought about it, might have surprised her. If Grace got worse, she'd get Angus's opinion. And she had Emma's mobile number if Grace needed her mother.

First things first. She needed to find out Grace's temperature. She let herself into the house, pushed the pram down the hallway to the surgery end and slipped the key from the concealed hook where it lived.

She found the digital thermometer and slipped it under Grace's armpit and held her arm against it.

Mia looked around. Maybe a damp cloth to cool Grace by evaporation while they waited for the thermometer to do its job? She filled a dish from the hand basin with warm water and grabbed the hand towel to rest behind Grace's head in the pram as she remembered that warm wipes caused better results than cool as there was less shock to the child.

She sponged the little red cheeks and around Grace's neck. Grace whimpered, but didn't open her eyes. The thermometer beeped to say it was ready, and she closed her eyes before looking to see what she knew would be a significant temperature.

Thirty-nine point five degrees Celsius.

No wonder Grace's cheeks were red. She'd hate to think what it would have been without the breeze and the washer.

She needed the dispensary. Mia searched for the key. She grabbed the paracetamol and a syringe to dribble the medicine into Grace's mouth. The half an hour before her mother arrived would be past before she knew it, Mia thought, and tickled Grace under her chin to encourage her to sip from the syringe while she dozed.

When the paracetamol was gone Mia brought the bottle and the syringe back to her bedroom and left the hallway door open. There wasn't much breeze, but she'd sit under the ceiling fan. Grace would be cooler in her pram than in Mia's arms so she didn't pick her up, even though she wanted to.

When Grace stiffened and then began to shudder in the pram she glanced at the clock to time the episode because she knew it would feel like hours, then she turned Grace onto her side. She wanted Angus. Mia didn't hesitate as she pulled her mobile from her bag and dialled the number he'd given her in Brisbane.

Mia knew the febrile convulsion was extra brain activity caused by the temperature and it would stop soon, but it didn't stop her own pulse rate from leaping.

'Angus?'

'Mia? What's wrong?' There was no doubt she had his attention.

'I'm at the residence with Emma's two-year-old and she's having a febrile convulsion. I know they're more scary than dangerous, but you have your car there and I'd appreciate your company and if you would bring Emma.'

'I'm on my way.' Mia sighed with relief. She'd known he'd come without hesitation. That even after what they'd decided, he would be there if she needed him.

After less than a minute Grace gave one final

shudder and then sank back into the pram and into a deep sleep. Mia's breath whistled between her teeth. She'd move the pram to the kitchen where there was more room for the extra people.

It only seemed a moment later when Emma rushed to the pram and peered down at her daughter. Her shoulders slumped with relief when she saw the little chest rise and fall in a gentle breath. 'Is she all right? What happened? I'm a bad mother. I should never have left her.'

Angus followed her in. 'You're a fabulous mother,' Angus said firmly. 'People leave sick children in the care of nurses all the time, Emma.'

Emma twisted her fingers as she stared at her daughter as if afraid to stimulate another fit.

'You can touch her,' Angus said. 'Actually, she's much cooler here than she would have been at the church, and she's in good hands.' The look he gave Mia held sympathy for the stress she'd been under, and it was incredible the comfort she gained from that one sympathetic look. Just to know that he understood.

Mia touched Emma's shoulder until the young mum looked at her and she had her attention. 'She's fine now, Emma. Her temp was thirty-nine and I sponged her and gave her paracetamol about ten minutes ago, just before she started shaking. I think she's cooling down already. It was thirty-eight just then.' She looked at Emma. 'It was more of the shudders than a full-blown convulsion, and she didn't go blue or anything.'

Emma looked from Mia to Angus and back again as Mia's words sank in. 'Thank goodness you were here. Imagine if I'd been walking home on my own.'

'I'll be back.' Angus slipped briefly from the room and then returned with a stethoscope around his neck and a pencil torch. He crouched down beside the pram and lifted Grace's little wrist in his to feel her pulse.

Mia turned away from the sight of his big hand so carefully cradling Grace's because it touched her unbearably that he could be so gentle. She knew he could be tender from that day in Brisbane, could be lots of things, and she damped down the memories of that magical afternoon. She needed something to do with her own hands and glanced at the fridge.

She made up three glasses of ice and lemonade and put them on the kitchen table. 'Sit down. Have a drink, Emma. You might get too busy later.' No doubt Emma would forget to look after herself with Grace sick, and the day outside was hot.

Emma tore her eyes from her daughter and looked blankly at Mia. 'What if she does it again?'

'You'll be fine, and so will Grace.' Angus looked up from where he was crouched beside the pram. 'It's common, Emma. About three per cent of kids can have an episode when they have a temperature.' He checked Grace's throat and then her ears. 'Most kids only have one convulsion, and if we keep Grace's temperature down, she's less likely to have another. She'll grow out of it. They're pretty rare after five years old.'

Emma slumped in the chair and took a sip of the lemonade. 'That's another three years!'

He smiled up at the worried mum. 'That doesn't mean she'll have any more.'

Emma looked down at her daughter and bit her lip. 'She's sleeping so deeply now.'

Angus nodded. 'That's how it works. Her brain is tired from the extra activity and needs a rest.'

'What do I do if she does have another one?' Emma chewed her lip at the thought.

'There's nothing you can do. Just make sure she's safe, not going to fall off her bed or anything, and time how long it lasts. See what she does so you can describe it later. You can't do anything else.'

'That's really scary.'

Mia hugged Emma. 'She'll know you're there if she needs you. It will only last for a few seconds or at most a couple of minutes. Sometimes they just stiffen, sometimes they shake and sometimes they just stare and do nothing.'

'That's right,' Angus agreed. 'If it goes longer than five minutes or she has another one straight afterwards, you need to call the ambulance to take her to the hospital and get checked out again.'

Emma began to look a little less stressed. 'So what caused it?'

'Her throat and ears are a bit red,' Angus said. 'It's probably a virus. The fever in itself is not harmful as long as it's not too high. Just remember if there's more than one fit we like to rule out anything nasty like meningitis, but there's no sign of that. Her neck's not stiff and, while she's unwell, she's not pale and limp with it.'

'Thanks, Angus.' She turned to Mia. 'And you, Mia, for looking after Grace. It would have been horrible if I'd been on my own.'

'You would have done fine,' Mia said. 'You're a great mum, Emma. Grace is lucky to have you.'

Emma took a steadying breath. 'I know what to look for and what to do now. I'm sorry you had to come away from the wedding, Dr Campbell.'

Angus smiled. 'My pleasure, Emma. The wedding will come to us in a minute, anyway. Did you see the marquee in the back yard? It's huge. How about I run you home so you can put Grace to bed?'

Emma shook her head resolutely. 'It would probably be quicker to walk and not have to fold up the pram. But thanks anyway.' She turned to Mia. 'Thanks for everything, Mia.'

'We midwives have to stick together. You would have done it for me, Emma, if our places were swapped. I hope Grace is feeling better soon.'

Mia watched Angus open the front door for Emma to wheel the pram out—the gentleman who opened doors and made coffee and treated women with that added respect, that touched her all too evident. She looked around the kitchen as if for somewhere to hide before he turned back. Of course, there was nowhere.

'It was a lovely wedding,' she said, and her mind went blank.

'Yes, it was.' Angus didn't help with his short answer.

Mia chewed her lip and wished the rest of the guests would arrive. 'Thank you for bringing Emma.'

'You're welcome.' Angus was looking at her, but she couldn't read his guarded face, as usual.

She needed to get out of here.

Angus stood there and drank in the sight of her. Before he could say anything the wedding party arrived and the swirl of guests through the front door separated them until he couldn't even see her. Maybe it was better that way.

CHAPTER TEN

LATE in the evening, when the wedding guests had eaten and the music slowed, Angus spotted Mia against a flower-decked pole, alone, as she watched the couples entwined on the miniature dance floor.

Her face was in profile and he ached to run his finger across her cheekbones and down to her beautiful mouth. He would never forget the taste of Mia.

The roof of the marquee was strung with fairy-lights and the trail led to the veranda where more couples swayed gently in the semi-darkness.

She looked up when he approached and he imagined he saw a welcome before she looked away. 'Will you dance with me, Mia?'

She didn't say anything, but held out her hand and he took it, warm and tiny in his, the connection between them so strong it was amazing it didn't glow like the lights above. He wanted to hold onto her for ever, but he knew he couldn't do that. Knew that the memories of his past prevented him from giving all of himself, and she needed more than he had to offer.

Mia stepped into his arms and slipped neatly under his chin, her body a perfect, incredibly sweet fit to his as they swayed with the music, and his hands wanted to feel again the silk of her skin against him.

He knew what this was, a farewell dance for lost chances, and he bent his head and kissed her hair and drank in the scent that was her because no matter how bitter-sweet it was, he had to feel her against him one more time.

And when the dance ended she stepped out of his arms as if breaking a spell, and without looking at him she walked away. The pain sliced into him in acknowledgment of the clean break she was giving him. It was better this way.

Montana and Misty had decreed that Mia should not be there to watch Angus pack in the morning and the idea of escape to a picnic with the babies was a good one.

But by two o'clock Mia decided the picnic had served its purpose—removed her from the house while Angus prepared to leave—but she was over it.

The whole time with her friends and their babies she'd been thinking of Angus, and that wasn't good.

She owed it to the child growing inside her to be a responsible parent, be alert to the dangers of falling for handsome strangers and stay focussed on their future. The future was her reality and the time for thinking about Angus should be firmly in the past.

Little Dawn sat quietly on her play rug as Montana packed up the toys around her, toys that Mia's child might play with one day in the future.

'She's perfect. Such a good little girl, Montana,' Mia said wistfully.

Montana caught her eye. 'Almost. She does love to borrow Jarrad's Wabbit. Andy bought it for Jarrad, but Wabbit manages to end up with Dawn whenever I'm not looking. And she gets outside and hides him whenever she can. Dawn loves the outdoors. I swear she knows she was born on a mountainside.'

Misty laughed. 'Remind me not to drive anywhere late in my pregnancy, then.'

'Me, too.' Mia laughed and Montana smiled softly at the memory. 'It wasn't too bad actually. Then Andy came.'

A blue and gold butterfly fluttered down onto the grass beside Dawn and the little girl's big eyes opened wide in wonder. Her chubby fingers opened and shut as she deliberated on how to catch the butterfly.

She was so beautiful, Misty thought as she caressed her own bulge, and then Dawn's little brother must have thought so too because he let out a such a loud gurgling coo in his stroller that all three women turned to laugh at him.

In the seconds before Mia turned back, in that

brief window of time, Dawn dashed after the butterfly and disappeared. Just like that.

Mia blinked and swivelled her head and a black emptiness opened in her stomach. She couldn't be far away, Mia thought as she scrambled to her feet, but the speed of Dawn's vanishing made her mouth drop open.

Mia looked at her friend. 'Montana! Where's Dawn?'

Montana stared at the rug in shock and spun around to scan the clearing. 'She was just there.'

'Dawn!' Montana's hands cupped her mouth as she rushed to the nearby stream, but it was sluggish and not deep and her shoulders slumped with relief when Dawn wasn't there.

Mia glimpsed another butterfly floating a few feet back into the bushes. 'I'll go this way.' She could barely hear the sounds of her friends calling Dawn's name through the thumping in her heart and crash of the bushes as she followed the butterfly that darted ahead.

She followed the blue wings blindly, calling Dawn's name, deeper into the woods as the butterfly left the green shallow basin of the valley floor and gradually began to float up the rocky hillside.

Mia began to stumble. Surely a two-year-old couldn't have come this far? But the idea of going back to Montana empty-handed pushed her on just that little bit farther.

Finally she popped out into an uneven gravel

clearing dug into the hillside and suddenly the butterfly disappeared.

Where was the butterfly? A sob bubbled up with her fear… Where was Dawn?

Mia wrung her hands. She'd been the last person to see her. She'd been sitting right next to her. It was partly her fault. She glanced around wildly and realised the clearing ended in a jumble of boards that crisscrossed the entrance to another abandoned mine. Not here.

She turned back the way she'd come and something shifted strangely under her feet. A sideways shift as she took another step and then suddenly, with a subtle rumble and a shiver in the soil, a crack appeared between her feet, and then a section of the gravel floor caved in and she slid without purchase on her bottom down a bumpy incline that opened beneath her in an avalanche of crumbling pebbles and dirt into a shaft below.

Just as suddenly as it started her descent stopped halfway down. She could still see the sky above her and the tops of some trees, but the panic she tried to control pounded in her throat. It would be okay. All she had to do was crawl back up the incline and to the edge of the clearing.

She brushed her hands shakily and whistled through her teeth at the sting from gravel pockets in her palms that she'd gained at on the way down. It would be okay. She hadn't hurt herself. She felt her belly and reassured herself that her baby was fine. No reason for it not to be.

'Help…' Her voice was shaky and barely audible and she swallowed the dust in her throat and tried again.

'Help!' Though who she thought would hear her was a joke. Not a very funny one.

The hope that Montana would have found Dawn by now kept her from dwelling too much on her own precarious position. Where was Angus when she needed him? This was right up his alley. The thought steadied her until she realised he was probably gone by now.

How could she have been so stupid as to think Dawn would have climbed this hill?

Which in turn would make others less likely to look for her here!

The panic built in her throat again and she squashed it down, along with a sneaky little hiccough of fear that slipped out no matter how hard she tried to hold it in.

Misty would find her. Misty was good at finding things and people.

She peered to see what was beneath the soles of her shoes, whether the slide went farther, whether there was actually anything under her or if she was hanging over a precipice. The though struck a chill that wouldn't leave and she hugged herself in the dimness.

The reasonable thing was to attempt to go up. She sniffed resolutely and shifted with excruciating slowness around onto her wobbling knees. Ouch.

She craned her neck. It was farther than she'd first

thought and anything to hang onto seemed to be as flimsy as her resolve to get started.

'Help!'

When Angus opened the door to Andy he knew something was badly wrong.

Andy whistled with relief. 'You haven't left yet! I'm glad. We need your expertise. Someone…' Andy looked away and then back again '…has fallen down an old sink, or a shaft has crumbled and pulled them in.'

'I thought all the mines were blocked off?'

'The girls went for a picnic. Dawn ran off and it got pretty confusing.'

'The girls?' Angus thought of the dainty two-year-old lost in the bush and winced. 'Your daughter's okay?'

'She's fine, Misty found her, but then they lost Mia.'

'Mia?' Angus felt his own earth tremor. No time to stand around talking. 'Come in while I put my boots on.'

Andy followed him up the hall to Angus's room, still talking. 'Mia was searching for Dawn. Misty tracked her to the old shaft and she's shouting out, but they can't see her.'

Angus tried to follow the story, but his brain was more focussed on the fact that it was Mia. In danger. Underground. He looked back at Andy. 'How precarious is her position?'

Andy shrugged. 'Hard to tell. We don't think she's hurt, but at the moment they can't get close enough to pull her out.'

Mia. Underground. Like Delhi. Those dusty grey faces pulled from the earth. Those breathless corpses he hadn't been able to save flashed in front of his eyes and his gut clenched with remembered helplessness. He banished the images quickly before they infected him, and drew a deep breath. Focus.

Hell. He just hoped no gung-ho idiot was messing with the site. 'What sort of gear do you have and who's in charge?'

'Paul, Josephine's husband. Mine manager, he's our underground expert. You know him. He's rock solid. They're setting up, but he said they'd wait for you.'

'Thank you.' He wasn't sure who he was thanking, Andy, Paul or God, but the fear in his chest lightened a little. They would do this. She would be fine.

'Wait.' He spun on his heel and jogged down the hallway to the kitchen and the old dresser that stood beside the door, and began pulling open drawers. It had been somewhere in here, had to be, right at the back, he'd stashed it before he left. His fingers scooped all the years of old papers to the front of the drawer. There it was.

He eased out a wad of folded yellow papers sealed in an old plastic bag and when he had them in his hand he closed his eyes and squeezed them, striving for a plan.

The old mining kitbag. He'd put that in the cupboard under the stove. He grabbed the pencil torch he'd used on Emma's baby from the windowsill and jammed it in his pocket. At least he had some sort of back-up if they had a hitch.

Thirty minutes later he was standing back from the edge of the cave-in and they were ready to feed in the first twine that would be tied to the rescue line.

The walkie-talkie was strapped to a small remote-controlled car. With communication open they'd be able to talk Mia through what they were doing.

When she'd received the first line a second would drag in the rescue rope once they were set.

He didn't know how he would start the conversation, apart from hello. What could he say? He just wanted to crawl over the edge and join her until they could both be lifted out. But that wasn't sensible and he'd never allowed emotion to cloud his judgement before. Now was not the time to start.

It seemed he wasn't as detached as he'd thought he was as he'd prepared to leave that morning.

He'd studied her position with binoculars from halfway up a tree farther up the hill, and Paul had told her to stay still with the megaphone while they assessed the situation. Angus knew this area and it had been one of the weakest branches of the mines and the most dangerous.

Paul had promised a tripod crane in from the mine by helicopter if they could find somewhere stable enough to lower someone down into the slide and pick up Mia. But maybe they didn't need to be that technical or take that long to start. If she couldn't tie herself onto the rope to be pulled out then they'd go there. It just depended how weak the surrounding ground was.

He glanced up at the sky. At least they had a few hours of daylight, but that raincloud wouldn't help things if it decided to dump on them.

Obviously if that happened, he'd be the one going in. He didn't trust anyone else. The centre of the cave-in where Mia lay trapped had radiating cracks that extended to where he stood. The whole edge of the mountain looked ready to fall in on itself and he didn't want Mia under any of that rock. He didn't want anyone under the rock except himself if it came to it.

Paul had commandeered the small remote car from someone in town when Angus had phoned in, and now Angus crouched, ready to steer it slowly across the ground towards the sink.

Thin twine was attached to the rear and it snaked behind the little car. It was a bizarre picture, a jaunty mini-sportscar with shiny wheels waiting to drive itself across a criss-cross patch of ground, watched by a dozen sweating people, but he'd used remotes before for tricky ground. At least there weren't land-mines ahead, as there had been last time he'd used one, but the weakened ground was just as treacherous to work with.

He wondered what Mia would think when she heard the little motor coming.

He looked back up the hill to where the observer was ready to direct them.

'Let's do it,' he said, and pushed the controls to edge the car forward. The whirring of the wheels turning was all they could hear.

The little car trundled with its high-pitched noise across the loose gravel, bumped over ridges of cracks, and then jumped a few wider fissures as it approached the side of the sinkhole.

'More to the right', the observer crackled over the two-way radio and Angus slowed the vehicle and turned it towards the midline of the crater.

'Should be able to go down the middle. It looks rough, but fairly stable and she's right at the bottom,' the observer said.

Angus steered the car wide out from the edge to give it a run-up before the infrared line of sight was cut by the ground.

'That looks good,' the observed commented, and Angus accelerated the little car in a small burst into the crater and hoped for the best.

'It's jumped the first step, and tumbling down the incline towards her, no problem.'

Mia heard the funny whirring noise approach and then a little red sports car appeared at the skyline and jumped in after her.

'Now, that's something you don't see every day,'

she said out loud, a new pastime she'd taken up to keep herself company as she'd become colder, but she gritted her teeth as she heard the wobble in her voice. 'Get a grip, you'll be fine.'

She watched the little car slew sideways and then hurtle end over end in a brown shower of pebbles to stop only an arm's length away beside her, the bulky handset incongruous on its roof.

Every muscle in her body tensed, but nothing else happened and she sighed with relief. 'Hello, there,' she said to the car. 'I wish I could just ride you out of here, but it doesn't look that good a ride. But thanks.' The tape loosened beneath her fingers and suddenly she had the ability to communicate in her hands.

'Mia. It's Angus.' The handset crackled into life and she jumped, the ground beneath her shifted, and she slid another foot down.

Her heart pounded in her ears and she scrambled in the gravel around her for purchase, but she'd stopped anyway. She tried not to hear the tinkle of gravel falling a long way farther down.

Angus's voice came again. 'What happened then?'

She eased the death grip her fingers had inflicted on the two-way during the slide and patted her chest three times as if to say, It's okay, heart, you can start beating again. She was over this. She wanted out.

She pushed the send button. 'Get me out of here, Angus.'

All she could think of at that moment besides her need to be above ground was that he hadn't left.

'It's good to hear your voice,' he said.

'And yours. Though you gave me a fright and I jumped, and the ground fell away under me again.'

'Don't jump,' he said.

'Gee, thanks.'

'My pleasure.' She could hear the smile in his voice. Easy for him, she thought sourly.

'Put the neck strap of the two-way around your neck so you're hands-free.' He waited a couple of seconds while she did that then went on. 'Are you hurt at all?'

'No. Just my pride.' She paused and shuddered. 'And my faith in tomorrow.'

'Keep it that way. Tomorrow will turn up.' There was absolute faith in his voice and she clung to that. 'Let's get you out of there.'

Another pebble skittered away and dropped a long way before it hit bottom. 'Let's,' she said.

'Okay. Pull the string tied to the car and a rope will follow. The rope will be your anchor line.'

She undid the loop and pulled the twine. She hoped the owner didn't want his car back. 'Don't like the sound of that.'

'You'll be fine. We'll try the easy way first. When you have the thick rope, just put the loop over your head and pull it under your armpits so we can support your slack while you walk out. If we have any movement in the ground from the weight shift, just stop, and when it settles, we'll start again.'

Great theory, she thought. 'What happens if the ground doesn't settle?'

There was a pause, which she didn't like. 'We'll do something different.'

Maybe she didn't want to know. 'Okay.'

Angus watched the line for the first hint of movement and when it started to slide across the ground the breath whistled from between his teeth.

Okay. She could do that. Thank God. He fed the rescue rope after it and though it dragged much more heavily on the loose gravel, it didn't destabilise the sink at all. There was an anxious moment when it curved to go over the edge and the tension on the rim of the sink crumbled the side a little, but she slowed the intake and it settled.

'Keep pulling, Mia. The rope's nearly there.'

'I see it.' He heard the catch in her voice and he wanted to throw himself in after the rope and hug her to him.

'It's okay, sweetheart, you're doing amazingly.'

'Do…not…give…me…sympathy or I will cry!'

'Okay, Sister Storm,' he said in a jaunty voice he didn't feel, but it was worth it when he heard the tiny chuckle float back out of the two-way.

'Too right, Dr Campbell. Now, I have this extremely uncomfortable rope under my armpits. Tell me when to stand up.'

'Not yet.' He glanced around to Paul, who with Andy and Ben was ready to pull in the slack.

Angus tied another rope around himself, skirted the sink, tied the other end to a tree, so that if needed he could cross the unsteady ground quickly and hopefully pluck her from danger if the far side gave away. He liked the chances of this working less and less, but they had to give it a shot because it was going to pour with rain any minute now.

'Okay, Mia. Slowly does it. See if you can get to your feet.' Paul was directly opposite the sink entrance and the way she'd hopefully walk out. From the angle Angus stood he could see the rope tighten and then lift an inch or two off the ground as she presumably stood up.

'I'm up.'

'Lean back into the rope so that it's taking some of your weight,' he said.

'That's a lot of trust, Angus, there's a chasm back there.'

'I know, Mia.' Now was the time to pray. 'Just slowly walk forward one step at a time. The more you lean back the less steep the incline. Position your feet with each step and move your hands up the rope.'

She didn't answer, but he could hear her breathing in the background. He turned the volume up and he could hear the sound of gravel shifting and pebbles rolling under her feet as she shuffled.

The observer in the tree came through on the other

radio. 'I can see her standing and she's moved forward about two feet. It's pretty steep. Steeper than it looked from here initially.'

'You okay, Mia?'

'Dandy,' she answered shortly, and nothing else. If luck held she could walk out of there and it would be all over in a matter of minutes. There was no reason it couldn't work, but he had that crawling, impending-doom feel in his gut that he'd felt before, in another place, that he didn't want to think about. 'Stop! Stop, Mia.'

He saw Paul frown across at him, but then Paul felt it too. The rumble beneath their feet and the shudder that was building on the mountainside.

Hell. It was all going to give way. 'Go Mia. Go. We're going to pull you up.' He waved at Paul. 'Go, mate. Pull her. It's all falling in.'

He edged in sideways like a crab, as if to slip past the irate earth without it knowing, but a widening crack appeared beneath his feet. The crack incorporated Mia's sink, extended to where he stood, flashed past him and to his tree, and the whole ground opened up.

He heard Mia scream and Paul telling the men to get back, and then he was sliding down the sink fast, his back protected by his pack, until he jolted to a stop when his rope ran out. He hung suspended between two tunnels over what seemed to be a vertical shaft and he owed the tree a debt of gratitude.

Thank God he'd tied off at the tree. There was

another rumble, several short jerks on his rope, and he began to slip again, then he realised the tree was being uprooted and was going to follow him down. Not good.

His boot scraped a wall and he pushed with his toe to make himself swing. A short swing and when he could touch the wall again he gave it a harder shove as he dug his knife from his pocket. A bigger swing this time and another downward jerk from above let him know that time was running out.

Angus kicked with all his force and managed to find a rough edge of a tunnel to cling to while he sawed at his rope. Finally he was free and he heaved himself up until he lay panting on the floor of the tunnel. He just hoped he hadn't been disorientated on the way down and he'd chosen Mia's end of the catacombs. He didn't fancy searching in the wrong direction.

Mia! The thought of her in the last slide galvanised him into action. 'Mia!'

CHAPTER ELEVEN

ANGUS snatched at the two-way around his neck and shook the dirt off it. He switched it off and then on. No light showed and there wasn't even a crackle. He cursed long and silently as he stared at it. He resisted the urge to hurl it down the shaft. You never knew when one piece of equipment might help another.

He'd just have to find her without it. He was a lot better off than she was. At least he had boots on and some underground tools in his pack and his torch.

He reached for his shoulder and shifted the weight of the pack until it was in front of him. It had been years since he'd packed this. Twenty at least. He had matches and flint in there somewhere and he had the maps.

She'd said she was above a shaft. He'd pinpointed the opening of the mine on the map and it was only a matter of feet from where she'd been. If the ground shifted, the most obvious place she'd go was downwards into the shaft. As long as she hadn't been pelted with falling rocks she'd have a good chance to be suspended somewhere down that vertical shaft and in fair condition. The sooner he found her the better.

Angus wasn't too far wrong. When the ground had shifted Mia had gone backwards and would have slid down into the vertical shaft if her foot hadn't caught on the edge of the horizontal tunnel she hadn't seen where she'd stopped before. The idea of that or the bottomless pit didn't take too much deciding on and she clawed her way into the tunnel until she was backed up against the wall, hugging her knees as she heard what sounded like football-sized rocks bouncing past down the shaft.

The noise was horrific and she squeezed her eyes shut and made herself as small as possible as she tried to disappear into the wall behind her. Gradually the rockfall lessened until finally it was more of a slither of slowly settling pebbles and the tinkle of far-off bounces as the bottom was reached.

She dug her teeth into her fist to stop the whimper that wanted to come out. She was going to die. She should have stayed in Brisbane and slept with Angus for the next two days. What was the use of being careful? She'd never see her friends again, or touch a baby, let alone meet her own.

She didn't want to die here. She didn't want her baby to die. Dark and alone and cold and hungry. Bloody Angus. What was the use of a knowing a man who dug people out of disaster zones if he couldn't do it for her? She kicked a rock that was digging into her foot and it spun out of the tunnel and hit the wall on the other side before it fell back and down the shaft.

She stiffened at the rattle of more rocks and she winced as she imagined another rockfall caused by her temper.

'Mia?'

Her breath jammed in her throat and she opened her eyes wide in the dark, but it was too dim to see.

She ran her dry tongue over the dust on her lips and swallowed until she could speak. 'Angus?'

She heard him sigh with relief so he couldn't be that far away. But how could he be that close?

Sheesh. She was stupid. For a moment there she'd thought he was down here with her. She reached up and felt for the two-way around her neck, but before she could push the button he spoke again.

'Mia?'

'Angus?'

'It's okay, sweetheart, I'm across the shaft from you in the other tunnel. Give me a minute.'

He was here. Down here with her. That was great. Or was it? Well, it was if he meant to be, but not so good if he'd fallen in after her.

'Um, did you mean to be here, Angus?'

'Move back into the tunnel along the wall a bit, Mia.'

She slid her bottom along the floor of the tunnel, not that keen to go farther away from the only source of light. There was a scuffle of rocks and then a heavy thump and Angus's foot knocked against her ankle as he landed beside her.

'Ouch.'

'Sorry.' A pack landed beside her and he slid down the wall until he was sitting beside her, and his hip against hers was the most fabulous feeling. That solid warmth drilling into her like the biggest security blanket in the world and she never wanted him to move away. Until he got her out of here, that was.

His hand came up and brushed her cheek and then he was holding her in his arms and she never wanted him to let her go. There was something incredibly solid about that embrace in the dark, the warmth and touch of Angus's skin and muscle under her fingers, and she clung to him until her heart rate settled.

'You okay, sweetheart?'

She sniffed. 'Been better.'

'Right, then,' he said, and put her away from him because there was no way he could concentrate while she was in his arms. It made him even more aware of how precarious their situation was.

She sighed and tried to speak lightly, but it came out with a wobble. 'You're not a bad bloke to know when you're in a tight spot.'

He squeezed her shoulder. 'Yeah. I turn up in the strangest places.'

She put her hand over his. 'I'm glad to see you.'

His other hand came in over the top and then lifted

to stroke her shoulder. 'I know, sweetheart. So how are you? Did you get hurt in the last fall?' He switched on the little torch and even that tiny beam of light made her eyes squint, but she was glad to see the light.

'A torch. Thank goodness.'

'We'll save it as much as we can.' He ran the light over her. 'You hurt anywhere?'

She hadn't realised she was so dirty. 'Just scratches and bruises. All the body parts work.'

'That's the main thing.' He switched the torch off and she heard him unzipping the bag.

'What about you? I'm assuming you got a bit close to the edge.'

He switched the torch on again and shone it on a bag of papers. 'Plan B was a fizzer,' he said as he unfolded the papers and traced lines with a fingertip.

She tried to make sense of it but it required too much concentration that she didn't have. 'I gather that's Plan C. I hope there is a Plan C?'

'Yep.' He looked at her. 'So you mean you don't want to set up house with me down here?'

'I like to have neighbours.'

She saw his teeth flash in the dim light. 'I could probably find some.'

She shuddered. 'I don't even want to think about what lives down here.'

'Enough small talk, then.' He refolded the papers and put them in his top pocket. 'I'm guessing your radio is out too?'

'Not that I know of.'

His brain had certainly gone. Paul would be beside himself with worry. 'Can I have it then, please?' She handed it over and he switched it on. It had probably only been a few minutes, but no doubt it had felt like for ever up on top.

'You there, Paul?'

'Angus! Hell, mate. Don't do that.'

'I'm with Mia. We're both fine. We're going to head to the west section of the mines to get away from the loose earth.'

He heard Paul sigh. 'I thought you might. Andy said you had some maps. You sure you don't want to stay there and we'll rethink getting you out?'

'I've got the map of the old mines. Crawled right through here as a kid. I thought we'd probably be best heading for the more stable areas. The top's too unstable.'

'Oh, goody.' Angus heard the quiet comment from beside him and he turned his head.

'Mia said see you soon. I'll get back to you as soon as I know which tunnel is the most promising. Out.' He felt her leg and thankfully she had jeans on.

'Not a good time for a pass,' she growled.

He grinned in the dark. This woman made him smile from the bottom of his toes. 'Just checking if you had protection for your knees. Saves me having to donate my jeans.'

'Yeah. Right.' She was silent for a moment and he

heard the faintest mischief in her voice. 'I could wear two pairs.'

'Not happening. Let's go. I'll go first and you keep close behind me.'

'So this was your idea of fun as a kid?'

'Under my terms it was. Not when it's life or death.'

'Thanks for that.' Her voice was unimpressed and he grinned again.

He guessed she was right and they could have done without him saying that. He'd been trying to relax himself because the stakes in this rescue were way too high for comfort. He could have done without the ball of fear for his companion that was freezing his mind. No emotion. None. He had to separate the who from the how.

'Let's get moving.' His voice came out brusquer than he'd intended but that was how it was going to have to be. Back in the forces. She was his subordinate and he was going to march them right out of here. On their knees.

Safety first. 'Where's your rope?' he said.

'Still under my armpits.' Her voice was subdued in the darkness and he called himself all kinds of monster for being hard on her.

But he couldn't not be. 'Slip it down and tie it around your waist, sweetheart.' He dug in his pocket for his knife and he could hear her wriggling beside him. She was amazing. A lot of other women, and men, would have been in hysterics by now. 'I'll cut what slack we have and at least we'll have an emergency rope if we need one.'

'But don't they have the other end?'

'Yeah,' Angus said. 'But there's a lot of loose rock between us and them and if we have to come back this way, then the bit we cut will still be there.'

She didn't like the idea of having to come back, but she had to put herself in Angus's hands if she wanted to get out of here. And the fact was, she believed that if anyone could get her out, Angus could.

She had to believe that.

Several minutes later Angus had swung across the shaft as if jumping a puddle. Obviously he had no problem with the loop of the rope around his own waist that joined them together. She decided he'd better not fall because she doubted she'd be the one who held the other up.

Because of the light from above she could see him across the shaft and she knew at any moment he was going to expect her to do it too. And follow him into darkness. There must be a parable there.

Not happy, Angus, she thought, and dragged her eyes away from the black hole in front of her.

'You'd jump a puddle that size at home, Mia. Don't think about it.'

She mumbled more to herself than him. 'I'd expect to get myself wet if I blew it, not dead.'

'You can do it and I've got you.' Angus's voice was commanding and she found herself poised to obey.

Oh, Lord. She did not want to do this. But even more she did not want to stay down here. 'Here goes.'

She eased out of the tunnel until she could stand in the vertical shaft and then leaned forward, focussed on where Angus was standing, and decided she'd just aim for him.

She jumped and Angus caught her and pulled her against his chest. She could hear his heart thumping like a drum in his chest. Maybe he hadn't been as relaxed as he'd looked.

She peered into his face in the darkness. 'Don't look so surprised I made it.'

His chest shook under her cheek and she realised he was laughing. 'Typical. The first time I could have actually seen some expression on your face and we're in the dark.'

He hugged her one more time then put her away from him to crouch down for the narrowing horizontal shaft. 'When we get out of here I promise you'll see me laugh. Now let's move. Before you freeze to death.'

She shivered. She wished he hadn't reminded her she was cold. 'Oh, goody. Another death comment.'

'Watch your head,' he said, as the tunnel lowered to crawling height again.

The next thirty minutes Mia didn't think too much. She shut down her imagination, clamped wayward thoughts, and just followed Angus through the twists and turns in the tunnels.

Once they had to jump another chasm and at

another point they had to lie flat and slither through a section that had fallen in, but the section opened up soon after into crawling height again.

The farther they went the quieter Angus became and she didn't want to ask why she could feel tension drifting from him to her.

And then, unexpectedly, he said, 'Nearly there.' She bit her lip because to talk now would give away how close to the end of her resources she was. For the last ten minutes she'd been fighting claustrophobia and as it built she tried to ignore the tightness in her chest and the nausea and light-headedness that was threatening to overwhelm her.

Finally she could see light. Thank God.

Angus stopped in front of her. 'They've closed it off. We'll have to detour.'

'Can't.' She could see a head-sized hole through to vegetation on the other side. It actually looked like some sort of nest. She had to get through there. She'd use her nails if need be.

Angus spoke gently, but he didn't make sense to Mia as the images of rocks on top of her crowded her head.

His voice came again. 'We have to find another exit. There's two large slabs of rock blocking the exit. No way I can shift either of them. We have to find another exit.'

'No.' She could barely speak.

'We'll rest for five minutes.' His voice was gentle, but it was no good.

'I can't leave that light, Angus.' Nausea rose and she focussed on the hole. 'I can't breathe in the dark any more.'

He shifted back to sit beside her. 'Take the torch, Mia.'

She shook her head vehemently. 'I'm not leaving here. I can't.' She glared at him in the dim light. 'Aren't you afraid of anything?'

He gathered her in his arms and pulled her head down on his shoulder and stroked her hair. 'I'm afraid of lots of things.' He sighed. 'But I've never been afraid of tunnels and earth—until today. Because of you.'

She couldn't relax into him. Couldn't get the thought of being crushed out of her mind. 'You must have been a bloody wombat in a previous life,' she grumbled into his shirt. Gradually her blind panic eased a little and she thought about his answer some more. 'So what are you afraid of?'

She felt his mouth on her hair as he dropped a kiss then he lifted his head. 'You should have picked that. In Brisbane. I'm afraid of taking risks with my emotions. Of feeling what we felt on Thursday. Afraid of allowing myself to care again.'

She thought of Brisbane. So far away from the reality of this moment and she wanted to be there with every ounce of her being. With Angus. 'Brisbane was special. Wasn't it?'

'Too special,' he said gruffly. 'I wanted to run a mile.'

She didn't get it. 'Why?'

He sighed and she could barely hear what he said despite the closeness of their bodies. He wasn't talking to her, admitting it to her, he was telling himself and she was eavesdropping. 'I'm afraid of trusting someone enough to think of settling down. I'm terrified I couldn't keep anyone happy long-term.'

'That's a fair thing to be frightened of,' she whispered, 'and no one can make you take that risk, Angus. You have to decide for yourself.'

They sat there and Mia tried not to think about moving. She wasn't sure that when the time came she would be able to. Maybe she could stay here and Angus could go and find the exit.

Right when she could feel the panic begin to build again, a noise came from the tiny jagged circle of light ahead.

First there was the sound of a twig snapping, then something shifted in the undergrowth, then, bizarrely, a rhythmic whirring.

She'd heard it before, couldn't place it, then she remembered. It sounded like the remote-controlled car they'd sent down to her earlier. They were out there. They'd found them.

'What the heck is that?' Angus peered through the crack into the bushes ahead.

'Mia. Come look at this.' He beckoned her up and she forced her knees to crawl forward until she leant on Angus and they both peered through to the outside world that they couldn't touch. The world they couldn't reach.

They knelt there with Angus's arm around her shoulder, and as they watched a golden brown lyrebird slowly circled the inside of his nest in a stately dance. He raised his tail, spread the fan, danced twice more and then stopped. He made the whirring noise again, perfectly mimicked so that Mia expected to see the little red car at any moment, and then he paraded his tail again in a stately fashion just for them. Then in a flutter of descending tail and rapid wriggles he disappeared.

Mia realised she'd been holding her breath and after a shaky inhalation she could feel tears run down her face. She shuffled back so that she was sitting against the wall. Angus didn't say anything as he slid back and sat beside her. His arm crept behind and pulled her in close so that her face was buried in his shoulder. She closed her eyes and replayed the images.

'I was so frightened today, Mia,' Angus said quietly into her hair. 'I've never known fear like it before. It was as if my whole life had been designed to gain the knowledge and experience I needed to get you out of here. All the adventuring when I was young, the years of rescues in far-off places, and the times I nearly didn't make it—all so we would make it today. It terrified me. Imagine if I'd failed you. But that's not going to happen.'

'I'm not out,' she said dryly, but the fear had gone. The panic and the dread had lifted from her and she didn't know if she'd suddenly become fatalistic or the lyrebird had really done its job and healed her.

She heard the humour in his voice and for the first time in what seemed hours she could appreciate it. 'Yeah, true, you're not out yet, but I know where we are. This is the strong part of the system. There's half a dozen exits not far away and we'll be fine.'

She looked at him for a few moments and saw that it was true. They would get out. And soon. 'I actually believe you.'

Misty found them at the next entrance. She'd persuaded Andy and Ben to open up the planks and Ben was preparing to use the loudhailer to call them when Angus appeared at the bend in the tunnel with Mia joined to the rope behind him.

'Thank you, God.' Ben dropped the megaphone and stood back as Angus waited for Mia to catch up. He undid the rope and then they straightened up to walk out hand in hand, both squinting into the light.

Simon rushed up and hugged his father, and then Misty and Ben, Andy and Montana crowded around Mia and everybody was hugging and talking at once, and the light was incredibly bright despite the drizzle of rain. And then someone threw a blanket over her and she was separated from Angus.

Mia looked around, but he'd been paired off with Simon and they seemed deep in conversation.

Suddenly she was tired and weepy and didn't know where she stood with Angus again. She tugged Misty's arm. 'Please. Take me home.'

Montana and Misty made sure she was showered and tucked into bed and she pulled her pillow into her side and hugged it. She stared at the bedroom wall and waited, but Angus didn't come to see her and finally she fell into a heavy sleep peppered with dreams of dead-end tunnels and tumbling rocks. She couldn't find Angus anywhere in her dream.

Angus had seen Mia go with her friends, he'd seen them bundle her away, and he knew they would look after her. She was safe now, she didn't need him. That was when he decided he would leave.

He wouldn't leave before he saw her, but when he opened the door to Mia's room she was asleep. Her pale face was scratched from her fall, her hair damp from her shower, and he sat on the edge of the bed and watched her breathe, and he had the visible proof that she was safe that he needed to reassure himself with.

She would be fine and so would he.

When Mia woke the next morning the rain was drumming on the roof, and when she looked into Angus's and Simon's rooms she realised they'd gone. The cupboards were open and the empty beds were stripped.

There was no one in the kitchen because Ned and Louisa, oblivious to yesterday's drama, were off on their honeymoon, but Misty had left a note to say she'd be over at eight.

It was almost seven now and Mia didn't know whether she wanted to see her friend or not. She dragged herself to the bathroom and turned on the shower. She didn't want to see anyone—except Angus.

CHAPTER TWELVE

'SO WHAT are you going to do about, Mia, Dad?'

Angus had no idea. 'I don't know.'

'Do you love her?'

Did he love her? Angus closed his eyes briefly then remembered he was driving. He loved her too much to drag her into his life. 'Mia's better off without me.'

Simon refused to give up. 'You might want to let her decide that.'

Angus didn't know how much more of this he could take. 'Butt out, Simon.' His son's house was on the next street. With luck he wouldn't have to think much more about this disaster once Simon was gone. He put the indicator on and it was only another hundred metres and he'd have the car to himself.

Simon must have felt the window of opportunity was closing because his words came out in a rush as they pulled up at his gate. 'You could move to the lake. She loves you, Dad. And she needs you.'

'Goodbye, Simon.'

'I've got your mobile number.' His son was threatening him as he got out of the car and suddenly Angus laughed.

The euphoria built and he realised how crazy he was. An amazing woman was waiting for him to decide if he was willing to risk his heart. He should be more frightened of not doing something.

He looked at Simon and the humour in the situation disappeared as fast as it had come. 'What if I let her down?'

Simon leant in and held out his hand for Angus to shake. He gripped his father's hand hard. 'Don't.'

When Angus pulled up at the residence it was just after seven in the morning. The last hours of driving had given him plenty of time to think and plan.

Maybe he could take over his father's clinic at the residence. Andy had seemed to think so and was keen on Angus taking over some anaesthetics in the hospital.

He could build Mia the house of her dreams, right on the lake near her friends, he'd be a real father to her baby, make up to another child where he'd let his own son down, and if they were blessed, maybe they'd have another baby or two. He was jumping ahead. Maybe he'd got the wrong idea and she didn't think of him that way at all.

He had to force himself to get out of the car and find out if he was right. Learn if his life was about to change in the best way possible when he knocked on the door.

Then she stood there. Like a dewy rose in a green towel. Framed by the door. Just looking at him.

Mia didn't know what to think. Her heart had flipped like the fish in the lake when she'd heard someone knock, and she kept telling herself not to get her hopes up. 'I didn't think you were coming back,' she whispered.

'I didn't either.' Then he said, 'I left something behind.' And her heart dropped. Despite the crushing disappointment, she lifted her head to hear the end face on. She wished she'd washed the tear stains from her cheeks before she'd come out, though.

'I left you,' he said, and she frowned as she tried to comprehend the mixed messages. 'I love you, Mia.'

She blinked and stared at him. That was straightforward. Had he just said that? Had she imagined it? 'What did you say?'

'I love you and I hoped you might have some feelings for me, too.'

'Some feelings?' Was he serious? She swallowed and looked at this man who had appeared in her life only eight days ago. How could everything have changed so much in such a short time? How could she feel these things for this stranger who wasn't a stranger who reached her in ways that no man had ever reached her?

'Only some?' His question was tentative and not like the Angus she knew.

'Lots.' She laughed and suddenly she was in his arms and his lips were on hers and she was home.

When they surfaced he put her away from him and searched her features one by one like a man at an oasis after a lifetime in the desert. 'Will you marry me?' Angus finally got out. 'Be mine for ever, as I will be yours? Please?'

'Yes, please,' she said softly, and he glanced over her shoulder as if finally remembering where they were. He took her shoulders and gently pushed her backwards into the house and closed the door behind him.

'Please, the neighbours,' he teased. 'This is a small town.'

She blushed. 'The shower's running, I was just about to—'

He smiled. 'So was I.' The joy in Mia just kept building. Angus was here and safe and very, very loved, and then he swept her up into his arms and carried her through the bathroom door like a prize and kicked it shut. Just like she'd imagined that first day. She started to laugh.

When Misty came an hour later she saw Angus's car out front and Mia's bedroom door was shut. She tiptoed out of the house and went back to her own husband.

The wedding was held in the same church his father had been married in a month before, and it was decked in pink roses and pale green satin bows at Angus's insistence.

Angus stood at the altar, flanked by his son as best man, and Ben and Andy as groomsmen. He faced the warmth of the congregation from a town he'd forsaken twenty years ago and had never thought he would return to live in, and it felt incredibly sweet.

He was home, no longer rudderless in a world of disasters, and he would be forever grateful that Mia had helped him to find that, but more grateful that she truly loved him and would be his wife.

The music began. Joyful notes from the bagpipes played by Ned, home from his own honeymoon, and the glorious joy in the pipes brought back memories of happier days as a child. A tiny dark-haired flower girl frowned in concentration as she began to scatter rose petals from her ribboned basket across the sun-streaked aisle in front of him.

A fluffy blue rabbit showed his head through the petals and suddenly landed in the middle of the aisle and the congregation coughed and snorted as they tried not to laugh. Dawn bent down quickly, retrieved Wabbit, and cast a guilty look at her mother as she hurried on.

Angus glanced at her father, Andy, who tried hard not to laugh as he grinned back proudly. Angus knew he would feel that pride for Mia's child when she gave birth in the home he would build for her.

Then Montana and Misty entered together, beautiful, courageous women in the palest green flowing gowns, and he could feel the pride and pleasure swell from the men beside him.

He glanced at Andy and Ben, doctors with empathy and caring for a town that appreciated them, deeply in love with their wives and willing to forge friendships with him that would last a lifetime. Thanks to Mia, his future would be here with these people—and Mia.

Then his bride stood framed in the doorway, her hand resting gently on Johnson's arm, and his heart lifted like the music that soared as Mia began to float down the aisle in a cloud of the palest blush-pink chiffon, his rose, his Mia, her beautiful face radiant as their eyes met and held for the full length of the aisle, until her hand left Johnson and slipped into his palm and he knew they were one.

Mia blinked tears away as she gazed into the eyes of the man she would marry in a few moments. She loved him. Completely. And she was only now realising that he returned that love tenfold.

'Dearly beloved,' the minister intoned, and together they drew a deep, calming breath and prepared to begin their wonderful new life together.

0909/03a

Coming next month

ITALIAN DOCTOR, DREAM PROPOSAL

by Margaret McDonagh

Gorgeous but shy Dr Ruth Baxter doesn't do relationships – until a seductive encounter with her handsome new boss, Dr Rico Linardi! An encounter that convinces Rico that he wants Ruth not only as his lover...but his wife!

WANTED: A FATHER FOR HER TWINS

by Emily Forbes

Dr Rosie Jefferson's priority is caring for her orphaned twin niece and nephew, not her appearance! But deliciously attractive Dr Nick Masters makes her feel beautiful again and this single mum finds herself wishing for the impossible...

BRIDE ON THE CHILDREN'S WARD

by Lucy Clark

Years ago, Dr David Montgomery and Eden Caplan shared a soul-searing kiss. Now, gorgeous doctor David realises that one kiss wasn't enough – he wants a lifetime, with Eden as his bride!

MARRIAGE REUNITED: BABY ON THE WAY

by Sharon Archer

The Campbells' marriage fell apart when doctor Liz's gorgeous firefighter husband Jack thought he couldn't give her the family she wanted. Now one miraculous night leaves Liz pregnant, and Jack's determined to be the perfect husband and father.

On sale 2nd October 2009

Available at WHSmith, Tesco, ASDA, Eason and all good bookshops.
For full Mills & Boon range including eBooks visit
www.millsandboon.co.uk

Single titles coming next month

THE REBEL OF PENHALLY BAY
by Caroline Anderson

Everyone remembers heartbreaking bad-boy Sam Cavendish – especially shy practice nurse Gemma Johnson. She's spent ten long years trying desperately to forget their secret whirlwind wedding, but Sam's returned to Penhally and is determined to win back the heart of the only woman he's ever loved...

MARRYING THE PLAYBOY DOCTOR
by Laura Iding

Seth Taylor appreciates beautiful women, so he can't wait to get to know his new colleague, paramedic and single mum Kylie Germaine, better! Only for the first time ever, Seth's smitten – this eligible bachelor finds himself wanting to put a ring on Kylie's finger and become a father to her little boy.

On sale 2nd October 2009

Available at WHSmith, Tesco, ASDA, Eason and all good bookshops.
For full Mills & Boon range including eBooks visit
www.millsandboon.co.uk